Ken couldn't move a muscle now. He was held in rigid telepathic manacles. He sensed a terrible tension among the aliens and felt Thayenta's fear as forcefully as if she'd screamed.

Briv plucked at the air again and a bit of the unbearable brightness faded from the brilliant blob of color. Ken could see it clearly, though he had to half-shut his eyes. The thing *behaved* like a prism—shattering white light into the spectrum.

Then Ken saw that Briv was holding a metallic object, a smooth oblong, roughly ten centimeters long. The alien leader's moss green clothing molded itself to his body, leaving no margin for pockets. Where had Briv gotten the metal object?

Plucked it out of the air, perhaps?

It made a crazy kind of sense. Briv had grabbed the air, and the lumpish prism had lost some of its glitter—and Briv had something in his hand which hadn't been there a second before. Then it dawned on Ken: the prism had transmitted the metallic oblong to this chamber from somewhere else. It was an alien matter transmitter!

ABOUT THE AUTHOR

Juanita Coulson has been involved in the science fiction field most of her life. With her husband, Robert, she edits and publishes the Hugo Award winning fanzine, *Yandro*. Her first story, in collaboration with Marion Zimmer Bradley, was "Another Rib." In addition to numerous short stories, she has the following science fiction novels to her credit: *Crisis on Cheiron, The Singing Stones, Star Sister, The Gates of Eden, War Wizards.* She has also written three gothic romances.

The Coulsons, and their son Bruce, attend numerous science fiction conventions; they were Fan Guests of Honor at the 1972 World SF Convention in Los Angeles and the 1975 Deep South Con in Louisville, Kentucky.

Juanita Coulson also wrote *Unto the Last Generation*, LASER BOOK No. 11.

JUANITA COULSON

SPACE TRAP

Cover
Illustration by
**KELLY
FREAS**

Toronto • New York • London

SPACE TRAP

A LASER BOOK/first published February 1976

Copyright ©1976 by Juanita Coulson

ISBN 0-373-72020-3

Printed in U.S.A.

CHAPTER 1

"Ken! Ken Farrell! So they finally let you come back from the boonies, huh?"

The boisterous greeting startled Ken out of his reverie. He blinked, recognizing the man approaching him. Reflexively, Ken braced for the familiar punch on his bicep and held out his hand to be shaken. The clock seemed to turn backward as he exchanged the usual meaningless insults with Dave Saunders.

As a matter of fact, Ken had last seen his former classmate in this very hallway, shortly after they'd been pronounced spacemen by the Academy, slightly over a year ago. They'd shaken hands then, too, saying goodbye and wishing each other good luck. They'd both been eager and and a bit apprehensive at the prospect ahead of them: their apprenticeships. Appropriately enough, this place was the traditional jumping-off point for newly-commissioned graduates. Decorated with a series of plaques and solidopic portrayals of Space Service's most illustrious grads, Pioneer Hall's centerpiece was a mock-heroic statue christened "Outward Bound."

"You look great," Dave commented as the two of

5

them leaned carelessly against the statue's pedestal.

"You too. Bio-Sciences treating you okay?" Ken asked politely.

"No complaints. Hey, I see Survey trimmed you down, huh?" The tall redhead winked and prodded Ken's beltline. Ken took the ribbing good-naturedly; his own big-boned frame didn't fit the public image of a spaceman, while Saunders' lean and lanky physique did. But public images didn't count for much in Survey Service.

Ken gossiped idly with Saunders, but his attention drifted down the hall to the door of the Dispatcher's office. What was keeping Captain Zachary so long? Ken had reported back from leave in plenty of time and the captain had filed their lift-off schedule with Control Central. Just a few final details, Zachary had said. If they didn't meet that schedule they'd have to abort launch and refile for tomorrow.

"Well, sometimes we get too wrapped up in our work to eat," Ken said, keeping the conversation going despite his worries about the deadline. "Sometimes it can be strenuous. But there's not a lot of exercise except on final planet checkouts. Survey's a soft assignment."

His classmate lifted an eyebrow skeptically. "Soft? Not the way I heard it. You're clearing ground for the pioneers out there on the farthest frontier— just like they advertise in the recruitment tapes."

Ken laughed and said, "So that's why you chickened out and transferred to Bio-Sciences? You shouldn't believe everything you hear. Survey's been a good deal."

"Even if it means working for Iron Man Zachary? I'll give you points, Ken; you sure had guts, signing apprentice with him." Saunders lowered his voice and inquired confidentially, "Is he really as tough as they say?"

One of the nearby solidopic cubes drew Ken's eye. The display was a three-dimensional portrait of Survey's first graduating class—all the famous names, many of them now legends: Chao Li, Greschovski, Noland Eads, R.C. Zachary. . . .

He was tempted to build on the myth, but honesty won out. "Most of R.C.'s temper is bluff, Dave. A lot more bark than bite. Oh, he demands top performance. But I appreciate that. In Survey we're in the survival business; there's no margin for mistakes. And R.C. Zachary's the best damned pilot in Survey."

"At least since Eads quit and dropped out of sight," Saunders reminded him.

"Maybe." Unwilling to concede the point, Ken argued, "I've watched R.C. touch down on planets you'd think *nobody* could approach. He doesn't jostle the most delicate mapping gear. That kind of skill is crucial out there in the Deep."

"I'll say," Saunders murmured, envious. "Must be fantastic—spacing out on the fringes."

"We're a long, long way from home," Ken said. "If we get into trouble it's months before anyone spots the signal for help. That's why I'm glad to be Zachary's second."

"Mmm, but I remember him from the training sessions when he guest-lectured," Saunders whistled and shook his head. "Can't be fun cooped up with a hermit like that, and for months on end."

"We get along fine," Ken replied offhandedly. He checked the Dispatcher's door again, his impatience growing. R.C. should have finished his briefing by now. He explained to Saunders, "We use sleep-suspend getting out to the frontier so it doesn't seem so long between planetfalls."

"Great invention!" and Saunders launched into an enthusiastic endorsement of the suspended animation technique.

Ken listened with half an ear. The latest technology wasn't much use if your captain couldn't even meet the lift-ship deadline. Where the hell *was* Zachary, the paragon Ken had just praised so highly? Surely R.C. wouldn't be wasting time in casual conversation with the Dispatcher.

R.C. was a "stickler" for routine. Ken mentally reviewed his just-completed assignment—twelve planets second-surveyed and certified ready for colonization. There had been no problem at all; it had been a textbook tour. In those months Ken had learned a lot, including affectionate respect for his superior officer.

". . . once they get the transcender perfected we can make our space warp jumps in one hundredth the time," Saunders was saying. "Imagine! People used to travel at less than light-speed!"

"Time marches on," Ken cliched, then brightened. The door to the Dispatcher's office finally slid open. Warily, Saunders followed Ken's gaze. Ken's disclaimers apparently hadn't convinced his former classmate that R.C. Zachary wasn't an ogre. As Captain Zachary strode out into the corridor, Ken tugged his uniform tunic into a neater line and said, "Captain, you remember Dave Saunders, from the cadet tour. . . ."

Zachary's acknowledgment was barely civil. His brow was drawn in an ominous frown and his lips thinned. "Glad to meet you, Saunders," he said, sounding quite the reverse. "Let's move, Farrell." Without breaking stride, he swept past the two younger men, arms swinging and jaw thrust forward.

Under his breath Saunders muttered. "Yeah, you sure have got a creampuff of a commander, Farrell."

"He isn't usually like that," Ken said, chagrined.

Captain Zachary halted at the corridor junction and glared back at Ken. "You coming, Farrell? We've got a ship to launch."

Ken bit off a retort. Zachary hadn't spoken to him in that tone for months, not since early in Ken's first duty-tour. He wasn't a raw recruit any more, and he thought he had earned Zachary's friendship on that assignment. Furthermore, it was Zachary who had caused the delay.

But he *was* the captain.

Ken threw Saunders a rueful parting glance and hurried in Zachary's wake. By the time they'd reached the shuttle ramp, Ken was walking alongside Zachary. He tugged at his blond thatch impatiently, trying to achieve last minute neatness, then asked, "Was there some trouble with the new assignment, Captain?" Zachary eyed him narrowly. Ken risked elaborating. "I mean, it seemed to take quite a while."

They stepped onto the slide belt that would carry

them out to the ship's berth. R.C. studied the backs of his hands for several long minutes and Ken was afraid the man would ignore the question. But at last Zachary's mood eased and he said casually, "Just talking over old times."

"I see." Ken wanted to take the explanation at face value. It would explain Zachary's snappishness; the man hated idle chit-chat. If the Dispatcher had cornered Zachary for a rehash of past history, it would have left R.C. in a very bad mood.

THE slide belt bumped them off at Berth Ten. Suddenly, there was no time for further questions. There were hatches to close, a hundred and one last minute checks to make and finally, clearance from the Terminal to code.

Any friction with Captain Zachary seemed unimportant now. Ken's pulse quickened. This was where the real living began; those months in space on his first assignment had proved heady, addictive. He had felt out of place and somewhat bored here on Earth, marking time until he could lift ship for the deep again.

In a few moments they would receive permission to launch. After rocketing out of Earth's orbit, out of the solar system, the ship would head for the stars. A distant sector of space, visited only once before by a ship from Initial Survey, was their destination.

Out there, Ken felt he belonged. In the unknown.

CHAPTER 2

Ken shook his head and tried to refocus. The ghostly vision had faded from his console. An instant before, large, black eyes filled with silent pleading were superimposed on Ken's mapping screen.

Was he hallucinating? A pair of disembodied eyes on board a two-man Survey ship? It didn't make any sense. Bewildered, Ken tried to clear his head of unwelcome fantasies. This wasn't the time or the place for wool-gathering.

"I *said,* do you have an update on that surface feature?" He realized R.C. had been speaking to him, becoming irritable when there was no reply.

Sheepishly, Ken punched a readout from his mapping computer. Ever since they had come out of sleep-suspend and started approach to this solar system, the captain had been tense. But now Zachary had a real cause to be annoyed. If he learned his apprentice had been neglecting duty staring at a pair of imaginary eyes. . . !

An electronic stream of data flowed toward the pilot's board. As R.C. studied the information, Ken attempted to make amends for his lapse. "The scanners read it as a constant, Captain. It's strictly a surface effect, not a weather pattern. Some permanent detail, but I can't tell exactly what it is, yet. We're still too far out from the planet. The features are blurred."

"You're supposed to unblur them," R.C. reminded him.

Ken stared at the back of the captain's helmet, concerned. R.C. was living up to his reputation. Until recently, Ken hadn't regretted the choice to serve under Zachary. He had been brusque but scrupulously fair—quite different from the image he was presenting now.

Ken cued his mapping computer once more, ordering the circuits to investigate the problem of the blurred area below. Orbital entry was coming up; there was no time for nasty surprises. If that surface anomaly presented any risk, they had better discover it now. Survival in Survey Service depended on caution and efficiency, and following the rules had saved Ken's life several times during the previous duty assignment. He intended to keep that score perfect.

He stared in amazement at R.C. whose burly hands were flying across the pilot's board, programming a retrofire. This early? Furthermore, this planetfall wasn't on the schedule, at least not on Ken's tape. He hadn't argued when Zachary had inserted planet NE 592 into the navigational computers: an extra survey stop was the captain's privilege. But R.C. was such a demon for regulations; this unplanned diversion to a world far off their route just didn't "scan."

The formation on Ken's mapper didn't scan either.

"Got anything new?" R.C. demanded abruptly.

"No. Not really. A dimension—fifty kilometers circumference at the widest point on that blurred area. It's peculiar—the computer says it should be coming into sharp focus by now." Ken projected the Initial Survey map beside the present view of the planet's surface on his mapping screen. "See, it doesn't tally with the old chart. That's a permanent feature down there, but it wasn't here twenty years ago when Eads made the first flyby."

R.C. turned to look intently at Ken. Behind the pilot's faceplate dust-colored eyebrows rose.

"See for yourself, Captain," Ken argued. He fed the new data to R.C.'s boards. *Let the old man draw his own conclusions.*

Ken admired that original map. Noland Eads had done some precise work two decades ago, and with crude, now obsolete equipment. Eads was the A-One frontiersman of Survey. He and Zachary were the only members of that original graduating class still living, and Ken had ample proof of Zachary's skill. It must have been exciting, back in those days when Survey was a reckless, seat-of-the-pants operation. Ken nursed his own dreams. Someday he hoped to walk in the same boots Noland Eads had worn—not a mere apprentice for Secondary Survey, but piloting the first ship to touch down on unexplored planets.

Ken leaned forward, peering closely at Eads' Initial Survey map. He did some hasty computation. Eads had made the first map approximately nineteen point eight years ago. That meant planet NE 592 wasn't due for Secondary Survey for at least another ten years. So R.C. really *had* bent the rules, shooting them off-schedule to this planetary system. Why? Ken had always trusted R.C. implicitly, but vague nagging doubts began to assail him.

That planet down there was bending rules, too. A blurred surface feature loomed up where none had existed when Eads made the first survey. What were those illusionary eyes that had danced across Ken's mapping screen?

He stared at a critical reading on his second-pilot's board. Gravity fluctuation.

A chill snaked up Ken's spine. R.C. was punching a retrofire program in fast, and early in the sequence. Something was going wrong.

Nervously, Ken pounded a gloved fist into his thigh, then flexed his fingers. He told himself to relax. He'd ridden through some tight landings before. Iron Man Zachary never damaged a ship or lost a man.

But was the R.C. Zachary now piloting the ship the same pioneer who had built the perfect record? Normally Zachary wouldn't schedule a planetfall ten years ahead of due-date. The Survey ship didn't belong here, just as that blurred area didn't belong there.

Was there any connection between the two facts? Startled at the possibility, Ken sat up straight, scrutinizing the mapping screen. Planet NE 592, Typical Class M: A melange of blues and greens and browns. It was a world of drifting clouds and polar ice caps. Except for that blurred spot marring its surface, there was nothing out of the ordinary. This operation should be routine. R.C. would put them in orbit and Ken's mapper cameras would chart the planet for a complete Secondary Survey. They would land and collect biota samples, check atmospheric readings. If everything fitted, the planet would be classified for Terran colonization. Ken had performed these same chores a dozen times, and Zachary must have catalogued hundreds of planets throughout his lengthy career.

An insistent sound nagged at Ken. It was an unfamiliar sensation, as those imaginary eyes had been. He traced the source of the buzzing. Alarms!

He gaped disbelievingly. The second-pilot's monitors were screaming at him, and in the lower left hand corner of the small screen, a red dot winked on and off rapidly. A rasping blip accompanied each flash.

"Tie in," R.C. ordered tersely. The pilot's words rattled in Ken's helmet headphones.

Ken tripped the automatic belting switch. Bands of safety webbing closed snugly about his survival suit. Suddenly he was very grateful that R.C. played things by the book. After long service, some pilots grew careless, not insisting on all precautions when they made orbital entries.

One of R.C.'s admonitions rang in Ken's memory: "The most dangerous time in space is when you're coming out of it—into orbit or planetfall. Too many things can go wrong then. Always suit up. That's your insurance."

"Three . . . two . . . one." Captain Zachary counted in unison with the computer.

A long burst crushed Ken back into his couch. Usually a miser with fuel, R.C. now spent it lavishly. His apprentice squinted at the monitor. That red light was still flashing, unappeased by the attempted deceleration.

They were in trouble. The reality of the danger twisted at Ken. Amid dreams of being a space pioneer, a new Columbus or Magellan, it was too easy to forget that every frontiersman faced death more often then he reaped fame and glory.

Ken had never expected to see that warning light. The ship's orbital plotting system screamed "Error!" Their vector was wrong, their acceleration much too rapid: a quick ticket to oblivion.

If they hit atmosphere without correcting their course and rate of descent, the two-man ship and her crew would be burned to cinders. Gravity took charge, dragging the craft down into its deadly embrace.

The retros finally cut out, easing the painful pressure on Ken's lungs. He forced out a breath, gulped in a fresh one. Glancing toward R.C., he wondered how he could best assist the pilot in this emergency.

The ship had adequate fuel reserves and there were no computer malfunctions. Why was this happening? Why were they falling inexorably toward planet NE 592, a man-made meteor about to take its death-dive?

"Captain?" Ken hadn't intended to speak. It had slipped out, the start of a request for orders.

Zachary grunted and looked around, smiling wanly. "We'll make it. You buckled in tight?"

"Yessir." That social form hadn't been used for a century, but Ken felt like calling Zachary "sir," more than willing to nourish any and all respect for the man's skill.

"Here we go again," R.C. muttered. Ken read the ominous figures rippling up on the second-pilot's monitor and braced himself. The retros kicked back in another long burst.

R.C. was on the manual override, prodigal with fuel, burning it off in great reverse comet-tails. The g-forces reddened Ken's vision for a few seconds.

And when he could see clearly, he glanced at his mapping screen.

With a start, he stared closely. It was unbelievable —eyes, a heart-shaped face, and two delicate hands. The image was crystal-clear for a moment. She held up her hands, partially framing the face. Slim, tapering fingers, Ken noticed, hypnotized by his hallucination. Her glittering eyes had no apparent division point between iris and pupil. They were as black as space, and as unfathomable. Her skin was palely iridescent with a greenish tinge. Unearthly, and unhuman.

Go . . . back!

There was no sound, and her lips didn't move. The impression "Go back" bypassed his senses and penetrated directly into his brain. This warning was without tangible form, yet more frightening than the flashing alarms on the ship's boards. Fear and a strong implication of terrible danger accompanied the anguished plea to "go back."

The woman's hands moved in an unmistakable

gesture, making thrusting motions, symbolically pushing him away from her. She was telling him to leave this planet!

What was this apparition? There weren't any women within dozens of light-years of NE 592. Perhaps she was a sweet memory out of Ken's own past? But he'd never met anyone remotely resembling this exquisite creature with the jewel-like skin.

With the retrofiring pounding at him, Ken tried to speak but couldn't utter a sound. He could form an answer only in his mind: "We're trying! You don't know how much!"

The retros cut out, and there was an instant of eerie silence. Then the image of the woman was gone as if it had never been. Was he conjuring phantoms?

A new light flickered on the pilot's monitor. Ken swallowed a surge of nausea. Not only hadn't the retros done the job, the rate of acceleration was increasing. Soon there'd be a third light. That was critical. If a fourth winked on, R.C. and Ken wouldn't be in any condition to react to it; if they were fortunate they'd be unconscious from the heat of atmospheric friction. God spare them the agony of feeling themselves burn to death.

R.C. was talking to himself, almost inaudibly. Ken heard the pilot spit, "Damn you, Noland." Then Zachary sighed heavily, steeling himself for an ordeal. He swiveled his command chair and eyed Ken. "We've got problems," he said simply.

Ken nodded. "Okay. What's my job?"

The barest hint of a smile tugged at R.C.'s thin mouth. "You might try praying. I'm riding the solar packs to give us one more really good retrofire. And I think you'd better send a Mayday."

Hastily, Ken unlocked the security panel and punched the S.O.S. package. That should take care of the automatic sequence, no matter how busy the pilot and his apprentice got. Ken recalled his earlier pain and steeled himself for the firing of the whole retro package. Neither one of them would be able to breathe. Ken glanced at the security panel, startled. "She's not functioning, Captain." He pounded relays, tripped cross-circuits, playing symphonies on the board to release the Mayday signal. "I don't get it . . . she's *got* to work!" His angry frustration shook the helmet speakers.

R.C. winced, closed his eyes, Then he tapped the pilot's console indicatively. "That blurred spot is a dampening field. It's eating everything, including us, if it gets the chance." His set jaw almost bumped his faceplate. "We won't have any reserves when I'm through, but we're getting down there in one piece."

"Landing?" Ken dared to hope out loud.

"We have no chance of pulling her free, not on this vector and at this speed. We'll have to ride her down all the way. It's safer here than trying the lifeboat," R.C. said firmly, daring anyone to dispute his decision.

Ken had no intention of doing so. But would the computers and the laws of physics be as cooperative? He tightened the safety webbing another notch and double-checked his suit's integrity. The planet's surface seemed to race up out of his mapping screen now. They were terrifyingly close, roaring past orbital altitude. Digits worked across the screens so fast Ken couldn't read them.

Ken took a last baleful stare at the mapping screen, at the blurred area that threatened them. A trap, sucking their ship into its gravitic maw.

Something else, to the west of the blur, loomed up. Ken couldn't quite make out details, but it almost looked like structures of some kind. And something metallic lay close by. Impossible. The planet was totally uninhabited, a virgin, primitive world.

"Coming up." R.C.'s breath whistled through the speakers. "Ten seconds to retro. Mark."

Ken silently counted down with the pilot. Ten seconds to retro, or to the end of everything?

Three ... two ... one ... fire!

Fire exploded in Ken's throat and behind his eyes. Pressure, grinding at his temples, his veins throbbing in protest at the assault of g-forces. He gasped, then regretted it; his lungs screamed for fresh air but he had no strength left to suck it in.

"Full . . . emergency," Zachary breathed out.

The mapping screen jittered, froze its last image, and winked out, dark and useless. The retros were yanking the plugs on every auxiliary power flow, draining the ship to its dregs.

Ken's hand crept slowly toward his second-pilot's board. Every centimeter he gained was a tremendous struggle. His arm seemed to weigh tons; sweat beaded his brow from the effort. Somehow, he touched the lifeboat coupling circuitry. The rate of descent was still fatal.

What good is a lifeboat if you're smeared all over an alien landscape?

He nudged the coupler and connected the lifeboat's power-pack directly into the main retros. They gained another few seconds of precious power to fight the gravity trap in that blurred area.

It might be just enough to keep them alive.

The ship was yawing, unstable, bucking against R.C.'s frantic override program. That invisible monster lurking in the blurred area wouldn't be defeated easily.

All the way down, Zachary had promised.

Ken felt as if lead were pouring down on his eyelids. Then a response shuddered deep within the little ship.

Would there be enough power? And would it be in time?

There was no possibility for a normal, vertical touchdown. The best they could hope for was a crash slide, if their rate of descent permitted it. Ken blinked and squinted at the board. The angle was flattening! Not much, but some.

Unable to speak, he winged encouragement at the pilot. Maybe good thoughts would help. R.C. mustn't black out, not this close to victory.

A piercing scream menaced Ken's eardrums. Atmosphere, heavy enough to heat the ship's hull, screeched as it raced over the Survey craft's skin.

The friction would heat the metal cherry red, then white hot, then. . . .

"Hold on . . . damn . . . you," R.C. gritted to the machine under his fingertips.

How could there be anything left in the retros? R.C. coaxed another iota of power out of them. Tongues of fire roared ahead of the ship, a fiery glide path for the tortured ship.

Steering, lifeboat, standard retros—all the power the ship had—was expertly balanced by R.C. Zachary. Ken's own words came home to him. Well, he'd *said* he wanted to ride backup to the best pilot in Survey.

The ship, a silvery porpoise diving out of space into an unfriendly element, raced toward the smear of the planet's surface.

"We've got to take it . . . now!" R.C. said, his voice a shrill crescendo.

The rending, toothpopping jolt of contact followed!

The ship tumbled through all her axes. Objects broke loose from restraints and flew about the cabin, metal and plastic confetti, whose sharp edges were capable of cutting through a survival suit.

Only the dim glow of the command console remained to light the nightmarish scene. Ken's stomach churned, and his mouth filled with the sour, burning taste of vomit.

He was smashed from one side of his couch to the other, flung against the safety webbing and crushed into the couch's unyielding frame.

A seemingly unending, topsy-turvy roll. No

Academy course could have prepared him for this. Human reflexes couldn't cope with so much gravitational chaos.

The little Survey ship bounced and rolled across the planet's surface, until suddenly an excruciating pain above Ken's right ear overwhelmed him. A red-white, shocking brilliance filled his mind's eye.

Then . . . nothing.

CHAPTER 3

"Ken! Ken!"

Words reached out at him from far away. The sounds echoed down a painful tunnel, gouging at a throbbing ache to the right of his awareness.

"Ken!"

It was louder now, and more painful; stabbing at him through the darkness.

He flailed out blindly, trying to stop the pain. His hands were caught and held fast. Slowly, consciousness seeped into Ken's stirring senses. He touched cloth. Uniform fatigues?

Opening his eyes, he winced as light struck his dilated pupils. Gradually, his vision cleared and focussed on the figure bending over him: R.C. Relief broke the pilot's normally solemn expression. "Welcome back to the land of the living."

"We . . . made it?" Ken whispered incredulously. His own voice startled him. He spoke like a man given a reprieve from certain death.

"So it would seem," R.C. released Ken's hands and straightened up. "Though for a while I wasn't too sure you were still with me. How do you feel? Any broken bones? Can you move your arms and legs?"

Ken licked the residue of his stomach's upheaval off his lips. Gingerly, he tested his limbs. R.C. had unsnapped the safety harness and now examined his apprentice for injury, checking while Ken wiggled his feet, probed his ribs. "I feel stiff," Ken decided, "but that's the worst of it. You okay, Captain?"

"A full quota of muscle strains and bruises," R.C. said. He noticed Ken's shocked stare around the cabin. "I know. It's a mess."

That was a woefully inadequate phrase. Two meters from Ken's mapping console, a jagged hole gaped in the Survey ship's hull. Sunlight streamed through the opening, illuminating the interior. The cabin was littered with wreckage—fragments of sensors and monitors, shards of oxygen-regeneration plates, government equipment and personal belongings mingled in hopeless confusion. Part of the debris dangled limply over that rip in the ship's skin.

Memories of survival training courses rushed into Ken's mind. "Environmental integrity," he said worriedly, pointing to the hole.

"The crash gave us a new airlock," R.C. said wryly. "You checked out the air for us." The pilot nudged what should have been Ken's face plate. Only a few pieces of plexi clung to the metal guard ring anchoring the helmet. "You got lucky," R.C. explained. "Eads' Initial Survey was accurate, and apparently there haven't been any radical changes in NE 592's atmosphere in the last twenty years. Still one point oh three Earth normal."

"Where's the rest of my face plate?" Ken said inanely, still feeling shaky.

"Scattered all over the cabin, I presume. I'm surprised none of the pieces got in your eyes." R.C. yanked free the toggles holding the ruined helmet to the suit. "It wasn't on the flight plan, but you played guinea pig. When I woke up, there you were with your bare face hanging out, breathing unfiltered air."

When the helmet came off, Ken explored that throbbing above his right ear. His fingers came away sticky with blood. Concerned, Captain Zachary looked over the wound and said, "It's a cut about four or five centimeters long. Not too deep. Sit still while I try to find the medi-kit."

"I don't think I'd be tracking this well if it was a fractured skull," Ken murmured. He turned his head slowly to watch R.C.'s hunt through the debris. For a short while, any violent movement would probably bring on an attack of vertigo.

"Here we go." R.C.'s search had unearthed an apparently intact medi-kit. The kits were designed to take incredible punishment. Anything a human could survive, a medi-kit could weather. When R.C. had scanned the miniature medi-comp across Ken's wound, he pronounced "Good! The readouts say no fracture or concussion."

As the pilot cleaned the cut and applied an analgesic spray dressing, Ken waited patiently. The procedure was moderately painful and cleared the remaining cobwebs from his brain. Anxiously, Ken asked, "How bad's she damaged?"

R.C. repacked the medi-kit and looked around the ship's cabin. "Bad enough. I haven't been outside yet, but the interior's pretty well gone. Damned little is in one piece, let alone working."

That sour countenance was revelatory, and Ken sympathized. After so many years, Iron Man Zachary had finally lost a ship. But R.C.'s second record—of never losing a man—still stood; R.S. didn't know how badly the ship was damaged because he'd spent his time worrying over his injured apprentice. Ken appreciated that, and his admiration for R.C. Zachary as a space pilot grew even more.

Zachary helped his apprentice kick out of the remains of his useless space suit. R.C. himself was already down to fatigues, and Ken noted a torn suit and dented helmet thrown in a pile in a corner. As he rubbed kinks out of his arms and legs, R.C. scuffled through the debris to the hole in the bulkhead and peered outside.

"We're parked on a ten or fifteen degree slope," he announced. "Must have rammed into a hill. That's probably what stopped us."

Ken envied the man's aplomb. R.C. talked as if space wrecks on uninhabited planets were an everyday occurrence. "What does it look like out there?"

"Grassland, some pink trees. Basically it looks as Initial Survey indicated." R.C. turned to the wrecked cabin and stood, arms akimbo. "All right. I suppose we'd better see what we have left."

A logical decision, but where would they start? Ken stood up, and nearly sat down again. His body trembled, unaccustomed to planetary gravity after a month in deep space. R.C. eyed him thoughtfully and poked through the medi-kit. He dug out medication for them both—endurets of gravity compensation drugs. That would tide them over until they adjusted to the planetary gravity system.

"If you don't feel up to—" R.C. began.

"I'm fine," Ken responded, squaring his shoulders. The pilot was twenty-five years older than him; head cut or not, Ken was determined the old man would not show him up. While the pilot checked the main monitors, Ken went over the communications console, trying to pinpoint the failure in the Mayday system. A brief run-through told him the worst. "Power readings are dead. Even the auxiliaries."

"And the lifeboat pack," R.C. added. Ken regarded the Captain warily, anticipating a reprimand. But R.C. nodded approval. "Right thing to do, and at the right time. Good try, Ken. That extra boost gave me the maneuvering power I needed. Without it we'd be smeared all over the landscape."

Ken started to reply with thanks of his own, but R.C. had gone back to the main problem. "See if you can spot a power panel; any part big enough to regenerate will do."

"It looks like they're all in a hundred pieces," Ken commented, but he joined the search.

Sunlight poured cheerily through the tear in the hull. The golden radiance of a Class-G star and a warm Earthlike atmosphere made this a good world for Terran colonists. But a pioneering colony ship

would come with her own supplies, to build and
sustain its people for years. Being stranded out here
on the far frontiers in nothing larger than a Secondary
Survey ship was quite a different proposition, and not
an encouraging one.

The grim urgency of their situation struck Ken.
The little ship was a deep-spacer, not designed to support its crew on an uninhabited planet. They had to
get communications operating and send out a Mayday, now.

"Here's one," said R.C. triumphantly. He dug
under a mound of broken plexi and clutched the end
of the power panel. Ken tramped across the clutter
to aid him. "Can you lift that end? Let's get it over
to the imput boards."

The plexi sheet wasn't whole. Several large chunks
were bitten out of the sides. But as R.C. had said,
any panel big enough to hold a regeneration charge
would serve. It would provide enough juice to power
the Mayday circuits.

Wrestling the panel to the bulkhead took the men
longer than they had anticipated. For several moments, they sat on the remains of storage lockers,
sucking in air. "It's going to take us a while," Ken
panted.

R.C. paced himself cannily like the veteran he was.
Finally he peered critically at the imput panel. "All
right. Let's get to work."

INSTALLING the panel drained more of their energy.
The tension, the crash, all had taken their toll. But by
the time they'd finished, Ken was enjoying the effects

of the medicine; his muscles were responding almost normally again.

He gazed dubiously at the results of their labor, knowing that R.C. must be wondering the same thing he was. Nothing had behaved right since they'd spotted that peculiar blurred area, including the circuitry that should have beamed the Mayday out into space. What *else* had the strange blurred area affected?

"If we could cross-check. . . ." R.C. muttered, slapping the panel. He stirred the crystalline readouts to momentary, fluttering life, then they died.

"The longer we wait the more chance a linkage will go," Ken said, quoting from the manuals. The pilot nodded, not commenting on the obvious. "That S.O.S. acted like something smothered it before it left the antenna."

"I know." R.C.'s expression puzzled Ken. There was no despair—Zachary wasn't a quitter—but there was anger in those hazel eyes. Was it something his apprentice had done, or not done? No, most likely R.C. was cursing the bad luck that had caused the crash.

What *other* nasty surprises lay in store for them on NE 592?

"We must have communications," R.C. said heavily.

Recalling all the earlier problems, Ken stared at the power panel. He wished he could see behind the circuitry and examine the integrateds for damage. But the engineers had designed this ship with every safety feature: non-flammable, non-toxic materials, the latest equipment, and all the interlocks imaginable. Either something would work, or it was broken. There could be no halfway point.

"It'll work," Ken said, bucking up his flagging confidence.

"It has to," the captain underlined. Without communications, they were a speck in an endless void.

They set all the safeties and checked and double-checked the interlocks.

The pilot slammed the last grounding lock into place and the two men stared at their work: a jury-rig.

"I'll try it," Ken volunteered, but not from heroics. Suspense aside, he wanted to find out the worst at once.

R.C. nodded, sitting by the panel. Ken kicked through debris to the pilot's console. His own was junk, but Zachary's unit was merely bent out of true.

He played a series of harmonics, tuning the systems, brightening when they came to life. "It's working," he announced. "So far."

The responses were a little shaky, but the console was responding normally. Give it a few minutes to perk on all cells. . . .

As he reached for the master com controls Ken paused, staring at that gaping hole in the ship's side. Odd. He could have sworn someone was standing there, watching him. It was a very uncomfortable sensation that raised hair on the back of his neck.

He looked over his shoulder, but the opening in the hull was empty. Nothing was visible but pale blue sky and clouds beyond.

Ken's stomach tightened with an atavistic instinct he couldn't name.

"What's the matter?" R.C. queried. "You all right?"

"Yes, just a little dizzy for a second." Ken fingered the slippery spray bandage on his wound. "It's gone now."

R.C. looked unconvinced, but didn't ask any more questions. Forced to lie to cover his own hallucinations, Ken felt embarrassed. But blaming his momentary hesitation on the wound meant he didn't have to tell R.C. that he was seeing phantoms.

But for a second Ken had known there was someone standing in the jagged opening in the hull. Someone *was* looking at him. He had seen the face on his mapping screen twice, before the planet, or that blurry area, had dragged them down into a trap.

No, he couldn't tell R.C. The pilot had enough problems without worrying about Ken's hallucinations.

Ken shook off his illusions and calmed himself by focusing on the com board. It had to be done exactly right, but there was certainly no harm in superstition. He crossed his fingers on both hands and reached for the "on" switch.

Tingling fire shot up Ken's arm and sparks erupted from both the console and the wall.

Held in the vibrating grip of electric impulses, he couldn't move. Somewhere in the back of his consciousness, Ken heard R.C. pounding at the imput panel and swearing, trying desperately to trip the nonfunctioning breakers.

Abruptly, the tingling stopped, releasing Ken's hand. He groaned and slumped forward over the darkened com board.

"Let's see," R.C. demanded gruffly. He'd crossed the cabin in a hurry, cradling Ken's hand in his own, looking for burns.

"It didn't . . . last long enough," Ken gasped. The tension eased out of him, allowing him to think and speak.

"Are you sure? It seemed to take forever to get those interlocks to trip." R.C. manipulated Ken's fingers, assuring himself there was no serious damage.

Again Ken felt that strange, peering-over-his-shoulder sensation. A powerful psychic urge made him turn quickly, hoping to catch whoever was staring at him.

The hole in the ship's side was empty, as it should have been. No one standing there, neither animal, nor jewel-skinned woman. R.C. gripped his shoulder and asked gently, "What's the matter?"

"Nothing."

R.C. looked at the rip in the bulkhead, unconvinced. "Then what did you *think* you saw?"

"I'm not sure," Ken stalled. The sting in his fingertips and his anxiety combined to stimulate both his nerve ends and his courage. Maybe he should tell the captain about his hallucination and solicit an opinion. But Ken's preternaturally sharpened senses sounded an alert. "Do you smell something, Captain?"

R.C. stiffened, picking up the same ominous odor. An acrid scent took Ken's breath away, growing stronger by the millisecond. "What in blazes?" the pilot exclaimed.

Circuitry simmered inside the bulkheads! Smoke seeped from relay covers and began to fill the cabin.

"It can't do that!" R.C. argued, a man betrayed by his own equipment. "It *can't*. The non-flammable cut-offs—"

Ken recalled the blurry area and the other things that had gone wrong. Whatever the cause, the crisis was very real. Adrenaline shot through his veins, erasing all pain and fatigue. They would suffocate if they didn't get out! "Captain, let's talk about it later!"

"Right! Go!"

By now they were both coughing, eyes filling with tears as their mucous membranes protested. There was one logical quick way out, through that rip in the hull. Ken didn't know what lay beyond, but he was past caring.

He and R.C. crowded into the jagged opening, clinging to the sharp metal edges peeled back in the crash. Through tear-blurred eyes, Ken saw a purplish-green meadow a couple of meters below. Was there time to gauge his jump?

Explosions rocked the ship's interior, and Ken sailed forward and down, blown clear. He relaxed, curling into a ball, ready to take the shock. As he landed on the grass and rolled, the impact knocked his little remaining breath away.

Another roar overhead signalled a much bigger explosion.

As Ken slithered to a stop, belly-down in the grass,

he flung his hands over his head. Debris pattered onto his back and buttocks and legs. Gradually the noise and the shower of wreckage died.

WARILY, Ken gazed about. He was sprawled on thick purplish grass, and amazingly, he was unhurt. "Captain?"

"Over here," the pilot muttered, disgruntled. The older man sat up and dusted shards of plexi off his fatigues. Then he and Ken looked at the ship.

She'd plowed the grasslands for dozens of kilometers during her dangerous, unplanned landing. A deep gouge in the planet's surface stretched to the horizon, finally coming to a stop here, nose first in an earthen embankment. Canted at a fifteen-degree angle, with her battered and drained power package supporting her at the base of the slope, the two-man ship formed a ramp of metal on the natural landscape. The tear in the hull was only one of the injuries she'd suffered; sensors, power linkage, lifeboat section, everything was wrecked. Survey ships weren't built to take that kind of impact. The gallant little ship was dead.

"It's a good thing we got out when we did," R.C. said, pointing. Fumes boiled out of the jagged opening in the cabin wall and drifted through big gaps in the hull.

Ken tried to think of something comforting to say as R.C. studied the ruins of his ship; but Ken's own thoughts were pretty grim. That was a big galaxy out there, and Earth had opened only a tiny wedge into an immense universe. Survey Ship Two 4004 was lost and not likely to attract anyone's attention for a long while. Considerable bureaucracy governed billions of humans on dozens of colony worlds. A Mayday was the only possible thing that might have earned R.C. and Ken a prompt rescue.

They hadn't been able to send one. Fate—or planet NE 592—hadn't let them.

Maybe it hadn't let them repair the communications system, either. R.C. was right; there was no reason for the circuitry to fry in the bulkheads. There was no way it *could* have! Yet it had happened. Ken could guess what the ship's interior looked like *now!* It seemed they were utterly stranded, totally without supplies.

In a year, Earth Central's master computer might spit out a tape on ship 4004. *Check: present location of Survey Ship, R.C. Zachary, Comm.* There would be leisurely cross-checks by bored programmers, demands that the computer trot through its files again to be sure. In Central Processing, that tedious procedure would take a month, minimum. If the computer finally confirmed that Survey Ship Two 4004 was indeed overdue, there'd be a routine hailing call followed by a lengthy wait for the missing ship to respond on sub-space frequencies, for the gulf of space to be spanned by electronic appeals.

But Survey Ship Two 4004 wasn't going to answer. Her communications system and the ship itself were a mess of stinking rubble.

It might take a year-and-a-half or two years to untangle all the red tape. Then somebody in authority would issue a standard order to Patrol: *"Investigate missing Survey Ship. Last reported bound for . . ."*

Such an order would be low priority, buried amid demands for peace-keeping on Earth's frontier worlds and the need to collar interstellar lawbreakers.

Well, Ken had known all this when he signed on. This was the frontier. The challenges were heady, but so were the risks involved.

R.C. tore up a blade of the purplish grass surrounding them. He snapped it tautly between his fingers and said, "Like it or not, Ken—we're going to be the first colonists on planet NE 592."

CHAPTER 4

There it was again. It had become more and more difficult to ignore. Ken paused while sorting through the meager pile of medical supplies he had salvaged from the lifeboat bay. Someone was touching his hands and sorting through the supplies with him, curiously examining spray bandage and a medicomp scanner.

But he saw nothing.

Dammit! He could almost hear someone breathing, almost detect a warm, live body next to his. There was a delicate, flowering fragrance too, competing with the lingering fumes of the shipwreck. The scent, at least, could be explained rationally; a copse of pink-leaved willowy trees grew on the slope nearby. Perhaps the trees exuded a pleasant odor.

But the other sensory impressions were unnerving and growing ever stronger. Again Ken turned to look, knowing he'd see nothing. R.C. was braving the fumes, poking about in the litter outside the ship's lifeboat bay, trying to salvage something from their disaster. Ken knelt in purplish grass fifty meters from the ship. He and the Captain had picked this spot as a likely salvage dump and a possible campsite while they got their bearings. The vegetation was soft and lush, indicative of the moderate year-round climate Noland Eads promised for planet NE 592. There was not a whisper of breeze—no logical reason why Ken should imagine he felt hands touching him or breathing close beside him.

He sat back on his heels, shivering. Was he cracking up? If he hadn't suffered the same hallucination a couple of times while the ship was still in space, he might blame these recurring hallucinations on his head wound.

"Why don't you show yourself?" Ken begged, then cursed his imagination. Who was he talking to? That jewel-skinned woman was a fantasy, the distorted recreation of some woman he'd met during leave.

"Did I hear you say something just now?" R.C. had come back from the ship in time to overhear Ken's remark.

"Just talking to myself," Ken replied, hoping he wasn't as red-faced as he should be.

R.C. squatted down and added a few more things to the salvage pile. There wasn't much to work with: an incomplete medi-kit, scraps of clothing, a few heavy tools. Ken opened the medi-kit and shook out another gravity compensation gel. The medicine was working well, fortunately. Without it, both men would spend too much time lying around feeling weak when they ought to be constructing a shelter.

"We'd better make everything last as long as possible," R.C. warned. "I couldn't save anything out of the food section. We've got a few concentrates, and that's it."

Ken nodded soberly and restored the gravity medication to the kit. Because they were wary of further explosions, they had established the salvage dump some distance from the ship out in the grassland, near the pink trees. The site was well outside the range of flying debris. Each had chanced several hunting trips back to the ship, neither staying long, because of the fumes clogging the ship's interior.

When he looked up, he noticed R.C. staring about them, and not toward the ship. Looking for what? "What is it, Captain?" Ken asked hesitantly. "Eads said there weren't any dangerous wild animals on the planet."

"No." R.C. was narrow-eyed and edgy, standing up to survey the landscape beyond their makeshift camp. A rivulet of clear water bubbled past the trees and along a dip in the rolling grassland. "Can you make anything out of that?"

Ken saw what had attracted the pilot's attention— a peculiar fogbank, drifted across the prairie. To the west, it blanketed the horizon completely. Like the grass, the fog was purplish in color, a pale, not-quite-translucent veil. "Natural phenomenon?" Ken said uncertainly, and R.C. shook his head in strong disagreement. The apprentice squinted at the fog again, then speculated, "That must be the blurred area we saw from space."

"How did you determine that?" R.C. demanded. "You know where we landed?"

"I have a rough fix," Ken went on. "I had an estimated distance and vector compute before the mapper froze."

"All right. Are you going to produce the golden egg or sit on it until it hatches?" R.C. growled with waspish humor.

Smirking, Ken gave in and said, "We're northeast of the blurry area. Can't be more than a couple of kilometers off the perimeter. It's almost as if we were pulled here."

His own words silenced him, and he and R.C. stared at each other for several long minutes. Finally R.C. said it for them. "I think we were. Believe me, Ken, I've fought ships through a lot of tough problems over the years, but nothing compares to that. Something in there is creating one hell of a gravitic force, an unnatural one."

He didn't continue. He didn't need to. Ken was thinking along the same track—if the blurred area and the powerful gravitic force had been present on NE 592 twenty years ago, there wouldn't have been an Initial Survey report from Noland Eads. Eads would never have returned from his mission. He would have crashed on this planet, just as R.C. and Ken had.

The pilot sighed heavily, accepting what they couldn't change. "When we're better organized, we'll have to investigate that fog and see what's in it. For the moment, since you calculated where we landed, did you also consider the daylight problem? How much have we got left to work in before nightfall?"

Ken did some hasty mental calibrating. "Let's see,

terminator's approximately . . . hmm . . . give us six or seven hours, maximum."

"All right." R.C. tightened the belt cinching his fatigues. His clothing was torn here and there as was Ken's. In a few months they'd likely be wearing native materials and pelts. The pilot pursed his lips, then said decisively, "Let's try to rig a shelter here for the night. Give the wreck a chance to air out. Maybe by morning those fumes will be gone."

Ken did not voice his worry that the ship might succumb to another mysterious explosion by morning.

THE men used the hand tools they'd salvaged as clumsy axes, hacking at the pink-leaved saplings nearby. Later, when the wreck cooled, they might be able to cannibalize panelling and plastics for construction use. Now they were limited to a slightly charred metallic tarp and whatever they could find for tent poles. The trees provided a handy lumber yard, if they were willing to work.

It seemed to Ken that the pilot was attacking the saplings with unnecessary vigor. The older man ought to nurse his strength, give the gravity compensation medicine time to do its job. Instead R.C. chopped and hewed like a lumberjack, venting his spleen on the slender tree trunks—a man sublimating anger.

In a way, that had been true of R.C. ever since they'd left Earth. Ken recalled the unusual surliness of the man in the Hall of Pioneers outside Central Dispatching. R.C. had snarled at Dave Saunders and

Ken, though the apprentice hadn't earned a reprimand.

A bad mood had been eating at R.C. Zachary ever since they had lifted ship and headed for planet NE 592: a world that wasn't on the regular schedule for Secondary Survey.

Carefully, busily trimming small twigs off a felled sapling, Ken said, "Captain, if you don't mind my asking, why did we come here?"

R.C. halted his spanner wrench in mid-swing. He'd been mauling a willow to untidy shreds. Now he gaped at Ken and growled, "What?"

Ken scanned the fog-draped horizon, the empty prairie. They were alone, and they were going to stay that way a long time. Formalities be damned. He might be a mere apprentice, but right now he deserved some straight answers. "This planet wasn't on our assignment sheet," he said levelly.

Breathing hard, R.C. rested the spanner and leaned on it. Encouraging. Zachary's temper had never been violent, but just the same Ken was glad the pilot wasn't in a ready position to swing at his apprentice's head. Outrageous questions sometimes got outrageous answers. "You questioning the assignment?" R.C. was using his well-honed commander's voice.

"The assignment wasn't on the regular sheet," Ken insisted, hammering the point. He leaned the pole he'd trimmed against some furry bushes and dusted his hands, considering how best to phrase things. "According to the data banks, Eads surveyed this planet nineteen point eight years ago. It's not due for Secondary Survey for quite a while. There must be hundreds of planets ahead of this on the priority list. So why did we come to NE 592 in the first place?"

The crash landing had left a network of bruises on R.C.'s face and hands. Right now those bruises looked very dark against a space-pale skin. "You're asking a lot of questions, mister," he said, without pique. A stalling technique, one Ken had grown used to.

Ken's irritation rose to a simmer and he flared, "After what's happened don't you think I'm entitled to—"

He gawked disbelievingly. Over R.C.'s shoulder he saw the woman! She had the same face that had appeared on his mapping screen!

Standing just beyond the copse of pink willows, she was looking intently at him.

Not a ghostly image, this time, she was slender and delicate, no taller than R.C.'s shoulder. Her clothes were the same color as the pink-leaved willows. In fact they draped and flowed across her breasts and thighs as naturally as the leaves themselves, as if she wore garments fashioned of living material. Her hair was sleek, close to her head, a green-black iridescence, shimmering in the sunlight.

Was he seeing a holographic picture? The woman moved slightly, her pink dress stirring as if in a breeze. The same breeze wafted across the spot where the men stood and tugged at Ken's torn fatigues.

She was real. Her skin looked soft, glowing, an opalescent jewel stretched over bones and muscle. Incredibly alien and beautiful! She was no hallucination. Ken knew that if he could touch her, he would feel warm flesh between his fingers.

The breeze ripened to a wind, tossing the willowy branches and dashing dust into Ken's eyes. He flinched, rubbed at his eyelids. When he looked again, the woman was gone, and R.C. was staring at the spot where she'd been.

"Did you see her?" Ken said softly, afraid to ask. He had to know. Had his hallucinations taken on life or was he going out of his mind?

He was prepared for scorn or concern. R.C. might wonder if the head wound was bothering his apprentice. But the pilot's reaction was quite different. "What *should* I have seen, Ken? What have you been seeing?"

"Is it that obvious?" Ken chuckled weakly. "I think I'm going crazy."

"I doubt it." R.C. wasn't humoring him; he looked solemn, troubled.

Relieved to have a listener, Ken began at the beginning—when he'd first seen the jewel-skinned woman, out in space. He concluded by saying, "And I saw her again over by those trees just now. Only she seemed real this time—three-dimensional, a living woman. Then—"

"She disappeared." No skepticism in R.C.'s remark. He studied the place where Ken had seen the woman.

"It's probably that crack on the head," Ken apologized.

"No, I don't think you're imagining this woman," R.C. said curtly. His sandy brown hair was tousled, and his jaw thrust forward, making him resemble a human bulldog. He softly pounded the business end of the spanner into his palm. "If you are, I'm imagining things too."

"You saw her?" Ken exclaimed.

"No, but I've seen something . . . someone else." Ken gawked at the pilot. This was a possibility that hadn't occurred to him. R.C. nodded and said, "A man. Funny skin, like you described. Glistening, shot through with threads of colors."

"A man," Ken repeated, trying to absorb this totally unexpected information.

"Not as pretty as what you saw," R.C. said wryly, his mouth quirking. "I saw him for just a split second. Almost to the instant we first impacted. I blamed what I saw on shock. We hit hard, admittedly, but now I'm not so sure. The image wasn't on my screen. It was floating in air, looking straight at me. Mean-looking individual, though it's risky to judge alien emotions by human expressions."

Ken had never met any anthropoid aliens, but he knew that as a member of Survey's first class, Captain Zachary had. He had encountered several humanoid races during Earth's early push out into the galaxy—races which were now mostly extinct, victims of culture shock and poorly conceived initial contacts with Terra. But these had been mainly primitive, apelike beings, barely humanoid.

"Aliens," Ken said, thinking hard. "Intelligent ones and telepathic."

The captain's hazel eyes sparkled, and he didn't dispute anything Ken said.

They both had memorized Noland Eads' Initial Survey tape. If Eads certified NE 592 as uninhabited by higher life forms, that was that. Before he had resigned and dropped out of sight, Eads had been the best damned frontier Surveyman the service ever had.

NE 592 had been checked out by an expert. There were no higher life forms, no dangerous predators; the climate was moderate, the atmosphere and soil samples nominal. Eads had left the usual monitoring devices on the planet. For thirty years, they would run automatically, watching for ecological anomalies or other untoward factors. When the planet's schedule came up for Secondary Survey a re-check would be taken, and if everything proved out, the world would enter Central's books as ready for colonization.

"Where could they have come from?" Ken blurted. "These aliens couldn't have been here when Eads made his Initial Survey."

"They're telepaths," R.C. reminded him.

"Oh, come on, Captain!" Ken said, choking on an incredulous laugh. "I read about those telepathic birds on MT5. And I believe the Capellans can do a few low-level telepathic tricks, like making dice jump or guessing which way a bird or game animal will move. But, teleporting across space? We're ten light-years from the nearest solar system."

"How can we know what they can do?" R.C. said harshly. "These *are* unknown aliens."

"Dammit, we didn't ask to land here," Ken said angrily. Then he glanced at R.C., remembering the line of questioning that had triggered the pilot's temper. Shakily, Ken went on, "Did we?"

R.C. shook his head, refusing a direct reply. "I

never fought a comparable gravity pull in my life."

"The planet reached out and grabbed us," Ken said. He put their mutual suspicion into words. "That blurry patch has something to do with it." R.C. stared toward the purple fog, and Ken turned to follow his gaze.

He froze, stunned. The woman stepped out from behind the willows. Her slender body swayed, her clothing blown in the breeze.

Hardly aware he was moving, Ken loped past R.C. He wanted some answers, from R.C. and from the alien woman. She had taken the first step toward him. He could do no less than go half way.

"Ken, wait!" R.C. roared after him, but Ken's mind blanked out the cry.

As he neared the woman, his fascination grew. Her hair was a jade and ebony rainbow, glinting in the sun, her skin as many-layered as pearl.

"Ken! Ken!" R.C. was panting in his wake, desperation in his voice.

"She's not going to get away from me this time!" Ken vowed.

A flicker of doubt crossed the woman's piquant, heart-shaped face. Perhaps Ken's headlong rush frightened her. Too late he slowed his pace. She had panicked and started to run away.

"I won't hurt you," Ken shouted. He caught her in his arms as the woman half-stumbled and nearly fell. Ken held her tightly but gently, afraid of bruising her.

In the back of his mind a persistent alarm jangled and shrieked. It was all terribly wrong. Something about the landscape was hazy.

It was the fog! Moving out from the horizon, it swept toward him, a tidal wave of purplish mist.

The woman hadn't screamed, but she gazed up at him with terror lurking in her eyes. Deep-set, beautiful black eyes.

The woman's struggles abated slightly, but she continued to push at Ken's chest with her slender fingers. Ken recognized the same frantic gesture she'd made warning him to veer off when he was in space. She had been warning him to go away from the planet.

Again Ken got the distinct impression that he could hear her speaking a warning directly into his brain, though her lips didn't move.

"Ken," and R.C. panted to a stop at the apprentice's side.

"She's real!" Ken exulted, revelling in the warm body he held. "Not a hallucination."

"We're too far away from the ship," R.C. said, and the captain pointed to the encroaching purple mist.

Ken's viscera squirmed, in instinctive rebellion against the abnormal. The landscape boiled with swirling, threatening mist. He sensed its danger without quite understanding why.

R.C. plucked at Ken's sleeve. "Let's get back."

"Not without her," Ken replied, refusing to release the woman.

"All right. But remember, my 'hallucination' wasn't nearly as attractive as yours, Ken." R.C. glowered at the mist.

"Come with us," Ken said gently, trying to pull

the woman along with him. If he could persuade her to come willingly, there would be some way of communicating.

Suddenly, she spoke, but fearfully, as if speaking aloud were difficult, or forbidden. "Sk'lee," she said, urgency in her voice.

"Sorry. I don't understand." Ken smiled encouragingly. He tried to project soothing thoughts at her, hoping she would comprehend. If she was a telepath she must be able to tune in on his brainwaves.

He was shaken by a violent chill, as a purplish eddy of mist spiralled up out of the grassland, looming above him. Long-dormant fears slipped from Ken's subconscious as in a scene from a child's nightmare. He fought unthinking panic, facing something totally outside human experience.

Without warning, six men suddenly materialized. Smoke gathered itself into tangible, humanoid shapes. Six tall men, jewel-skinned and black eyed, circled Ken and R.C. and the woman.

"Not just telepathic!" R.C. yelled. "They can teleport themselves!"

"*She* didn't," Ken said frantically, turning this way and that, trying to see an opening in the closing circle of alien men.

"We've got to run for it!" R.C. insisted. The woman thrust her hands hard against Ken's chest, seconding that idea.

"Okay!" sighed Ken. There would be time enough later to re-establish a friendship!

Dodging this way and that, Ken and R.C. did their best broken-field galloping, trying to avoid the hands that clutched at them. One of those hands snagged Ken's torn fatigues, throwing him backwards. Ken lashed out with fists and feet, aiming where it would do the most damage. But the man's powerful grip and agility made it difficult for Ken to escape or counterattack. Finally, Ken feinted and launched a murderous kick at the alien's groin. He didn't connect, but apparently the threat was strong enough to catch the stern alien off guard. His grasp on Ken's fatigues loosened and the apprentice tore free, leaving a sleeve behind him.

Ken raced to the site where he had been cutting saplings, grabbing up the tool he had used as an axe. Ready to fend off attack, he spun on his heel.

The purple mist engulfed him, swallowing grass and trees and sky. Ken blinked, his orientation gone. Fog nibbled at the pink fronds of the willows now. Another few seconds and he'd be completely blind, wrapped in purple mist.

To his left R.C. was swinging the spanner wrench wildly, striking at phantoms.

Ken followed suit, slinging his makeshift axe in wide arcs. How could he hit what he couldn't see? If the alien men could teleport themselves from one location to another, they could teleport out of the path of the Earthmen's weapons.

"What the—?" R.C. doubled over, on his knees, clutching his midriff. He was gasping, as if he'd been punched hard in the belly.

And the spanner wrench leaped out of R.C.'s hands and sailed through the foggy air—straight for Ken's head!

manipulate a mysterious fog and create confusion in human minds would not need conventional weapons.

Ken inhaled a sweet, unusual scent. Despite his pain and his dread of what might lie in store for him, he was very aware of her close fragrance.

No!

Telepathic negatives, flung back and forth. Was he eavesdropping as they conversed mentally?

As the big alien male stood in front of him, his visage relentless and his body tensed with fury, Ken recalled R.C.'s description of him. Conflict must be avoided if at all possible. The alien was taller than Ken, lean and muscular, with a bony face. His full lips were untouched by the slightest suggestion of a smile.

He seemed clad in moss, a dark green material that wasn't a material. Like the woman's clothes, his appeared to be living fabric, part of the planet's natural abundance. Was it possible they could re-shape plants to their own uses?

"No!"

This time the woman had spoken aloud! The language wasn't Terran, yet Ken understood her. The sound was sharp and guttural, out of keeping with the woman's soft voice.

The big male responded in the same harsh grating language.

Ken couldn't follow the floods of alien words, but he understood the general drift of the argument. The woman was appealing to the tall male's better nature.

Did he have one?

"Briv, fytyina . . ." Ken listened quietly as the

woman played devil's advocate against her own species.

Briv. Was that his name? It suited him: short and unsweet and very pointed.

Briv was unmoved by the woman's plea. Brusquely, he swept out a long arm and brushed her aside. Ken had expected a telepath to be less physical, but these telepaths had proved to be violent ever since they had first appeared out of nothing and attacked the two Surveymen.

As Briv stared balefully at him, Ken felt an imaginary block of ice encasing his heart. He locked stares with him, and a powerful image hammered its way into Ken's brain, forcing itself upon his mind: a drama performed on an alien stage, without words or captions. But its meaning was as unmistakable as Briv's rough rejection of the little female.

He visualized one of the jewel-skinned aliens, soaked in blood, lying on a white surface. The blood seeped from his mouth and from a hideous wound in the chest. Ken understood that the alien was dead, and that he had died violently. The wounds appeared chillingly familiar, like something Ken had seen on a training tape.

It was a needler! A Patrol weapon banned to civilians, too cruel and inhumane for hunting purposes. The weapon was designed for war. Ken's stomach tightened. A needler was a *Terran* weapon.

As if in response to his thought, another figure moved onto the stage of that telepathic drama unfolding in his brain. A man, features oddly indistinct, moved to confront the alien who would later lie dead.

In the Terran's hand was a silvery object—a needler. Ken had guessed right. He witnessed the meeting: as the alien turned to flee, the needler flashed, striking the unarmed victim.

Then the terrible images evaporated and his mind was his own once more. He was staring at Briv, thrown back into present reality. Briv pointed at Ken accusingly and began to speak. The syllables meant nothing to him, but the meaning with its inherent accusation was clear. Borne along on strong emotions and a few final images were anger, grief, shock, incredulous disbelief, and the fierce demand for revenge.

One of the woman's people had been killed by a Terran, and with an outlawed weapon. The implications of that chilled Ken.

Briv concluded his tirade with a snarled, emphatic, "Gr'shaak!"

Bloody images and furious emotions pounded at Ken, combining into a staggering whole. In the eyes of the aliens, Ken and R.C. were one and the same with the faceless, needler-armed Terran. There was no debate. Briv had declared the hapless Surveymen murderers.

CHAPTER 5

Ken couldn't concentrate; his thoughts were scattered and disorganized. Either the psychic assault or the shock of the crash landing had wearied and weakened him. He tried to brace himself to fight back, but the aliens refused to allow it on his terms. Ken was outnumbered and certainly outclassed telepathically. He was no match for Briv and his troops.

What were the best survival techniques to employ when a man was really up against superior odds? In this case, Ken decided to cooperate, on a minimal basis. He wouldn't crawl, but he was in no position to stage a rally, either.

He had to communicate with them, somehow. Collecting his battered senses, he formed a countering image in his mind, hoping Briv would read it and understand. Ken painted his own reaction to the alien's murder—revulsion, horror, a wish to see the murderer punished.

The unaccustomed effort exhausted him. His knees buckled as he released the image and returned to the real world. They had to see that the two Surveymen were not conspirators of the unknown Terran killer!

The fog was closing in again, and Briv's expression, veiled by mist, seemed as unfriendly as ever. It looked as though Ken had failed. He was tempted to sink into lethargy, let them do what they would with him. The alien men circled him, grabbing Ken's arms. He toyed with the idea of making himself a dead weight, forcing them to drag him. Why should he make it easy for them?

But their grip wasn't cruel. Firm, but not painful. They were supporting him as well as preventing him from escaping. Could they sense that the Earthman was on the verge of collapse?

The mist filled his nostrils like a narcotic, but Ken stubbornly held onto his thread of awareness. He had to keep track of what happened and where they went, in case an opportunity for escape arose.

He was being "walked" like a drunk, forward into the thickest part of the purple mist. West. Southwest. Yes, that "felt" right to Ken. He had to keep directions straight.

Stumbling along, he opened his mind, and Ken could eavesdrop on the aliens' emotions. Right now, those signalled impatience and urgency.

"R.C.?" Ken called. Unless heavy breathing and the shuffle of feet constituted a reply, there was no response. Maybe they were dragging R.C. along with them too. If they hadn't killed the pilot. There was no real reason why they should have. Apparently they were taking live captives today.

The fog seeped in his throat and lungs, and Ken coughed spasmodically. His pants were soaked through and the fatigues chafed along the tops of his boots. Wet grass. It seemed to be a world of all-pervading dampness.

How long would this voyage go on? It was impossible to judge how far they had come. Vision and hearing helped not at all.

A momentary lurch turned Ken's stomach, and for a few beats of his pulse, his feet weren't touching the ground. He couldn't feel . . . anything! Not even the aliens' hands gripped his arms.

The sensation jolted him, badly. Another pulse beat later, everything was as before—aliens marching him along through the mist, all the sounds and tactile information Ken expected.

It happened again! It was like stepping in and out of the real world and back again. The process was repeated several times. He would grow weary, mesmerized by the fog and invisibility, his alertness melting into semi-consciousness. Then a jerk in the pit of his stomach would signal absolute nothingness; and then . . . normalcy again.

Jumps. The idea came out of nowhere, suddenly. They were jumping forward in space, telepathically. The aliens transported their human captives by tele-kinetic skills of some kind! Ken had read about such things in fiction, but never dreamed he'd be fortunate enough to ride an alien brainwave. Fortunate! He was a man without a choice in the matter.

THEY had stopped. Ken carefully shook his head to clear the fog from his thoughts. The cut on his head was tender.

The terrain had changed. The swish of grass and the scrape of feet were replaced by the echo of rock sliding across rock: a brittle, resonant noise.

After more clambering on the rocky surface, Ken was thrust forward. Something white loomed out of the fog ahead of him: a wall. A massive chunk of sheered limestone rose up. Abutting it was some artificial substance. It felt like plastic to the touch, but it undulated as Ken leaned into it.

Simultaneously the hands that had been supporting and restraining him let go. Ken toppled against the limestone and plastic wall.

He squirmed around, bracing himself against the rock. The fog had disappeared and so had the aliens. He was alone in a chamber built of rock and rippling white material.

A prison cell. There were no doors or windows; there was no entrance of any kind that Ken could see.

Ken slowly slid down until he was sitting, his back propped against the limestone. He surveyed his quarters: a rough hexagon about three meters across with no furniture of any kind. Maybe the aliens created their own out of their thoughts and assumed any prisoners would do the same. They wouldn't realize that human creative powers were limited to a somewhat more solid technology.

He caressed the undulating white wall. It seemed alive, yet not alive. For all he could tell, it might be mist, bleached and reformed, something the aliens reshaped at will. Did that make it a manufactured substance? He was a member of Survey, and this was the product of a previously unknown culture. That meant it was Ken's job to explore and note.

Exploring and examining would keep his thoughts off unpleasant possibilities. But all his sophisticated equipment designed for examining new objects and cultures lay back in the wrecked ship, wherever it was.

Ken sniffed the white material, wet a fingertip and touched the wall, then gingerly tasted. Although it lacked the distinctive chalky texture associated with Terran plastics, it was strongly reminiscent of that substance.

Briv's plastic. That's what it was. Briv was the apparent leader of the aliens, and this was an alien material. . . .

Where was R.C.? In a similar prison cell? Ken's imagination conjured up a horrible picture of the captain lying dead on a white slab, a sacrifice to atone for the murder of one of the aliens. He shoved the nightmare aside.

He stood up and walked around the room, kicking at the walls. No chinks appeared. It was solid. Where the hell was the door? Both plastic and rock were slightly warm to the touch, approximately matching human body temperature: a nice gesture, if it was Ken's comfort they were thinking of.

His head hurt, and he rubbed his temples rhythmically. There seemed to be no way out, or none that a mere human could comprehend. Until they chose to release him, he was trapped—sealed inside, the rest of the universe, outside.

Ken sat down again, heaved a sigh, and closed his eyes as he leaned back. It was futile to hammer against an unbreakable wall, so he took the opportunity to rest.

IT seemed no more than a moment, but Ken realized he'd been asleep possibly for an hour or more. He was awake instantly, but without exhibiting any signs of his wakefulness—a trick he had acquired when he was a kid. It was useful now. Ken maintained a slow, regular breathing pattern and kept his eyes closed.

Someone was in the hexagonal room with him. Someone had found a door, which meant whoever it was knew the secrets of this place: an alien.

He heard quiet movements, light footsteps, the sound of an object being placed on the floor in front of him. Still Ken feigned sleep. Then, he was pinched —a playful tweaking of the flesh on his forearm.

Startled, Ken opened his eyes and met those of the little alien woman. Her pretty face was devoid of any expression, but her eyes sparkled with amusement. She had known he wasn't asleep. Of course. He wouldn't be able to conceal it from a telepath.

She pointed to a spongy bowl at Ken's feet. It was heaped with exotic fruits that Ken recognized as some of the varieties from Noland Eads' Initial Survey tape. She was offering him the harvest of NE 592.

Eads' tape had assured him that these native fruits were edible, non-toxic. Ken selected one and bit into it. It tasted succulent, but wasn't going to be very filling.

The woman studied him intently while he ate. Ken

felt like a bug under a scientist's microscan. He shrugged aside resentment. She was bound to be curious, but he did wonder if she was reading his mind as thoroughly as she was studying him visually.

Did he dare seize her as a hostage and attempt to bargain his way out of this mess? It was idiocy to consider it. Briv and his troops would smash Ken down with a telepathic attack, some non-physical weapon a human couldn't even see. No, manhandling and brawn would not solve the problem.

She was staring at him, as she had when Ken was in space, though the frightful urgency in her manner was gone. There was little point in warning him of dangers now. He had already stumbled headlong into these, and the situation was considerably altered.

Again he wondered if she was reading his mind. How could he express his distaste for that? Images seemed to work. He built a mental picture of a fortress and raised it around his own head. It was crude, but perhaps she would understand and respect his privacy.

Communication was the barricade separating them. Ken had never dealt face to face with a highly intelligent telepathic species. No human had until now. He would have to deal with the situation as he went along. The Survey ship had carried a basic computer-translator—just in case the need arose. But the translator was smashed, like everything else in the ship. That left Ken deaf and dumb in any conversation.

He decided to go back to the beginning. He smiled, beaming friendly "vibes" at the woman. Still smiling, he pointed to himself and said carefully, "Ken Farrell. Ken Far . . . rell." He waited for that to soak in, then pointed to the woman.

She didn't say anything. Instead she got to her feet and walked around him at a leisurely pace. Was she looking for a weak spot in his mental armor? He had plenty of those!

Finally she stopped and knelt down in front of him again, waiting expectantly. Ken was frustrated. What was he supposed to do? Apparently the aliens followed a particular ritual, and she'd done her part in circumnavigating him. Sighing, Ken got up, duplicated her circling routine, came back to where he'd been, and sat down facing her.

Still she didn't speak or offer any communication that Ken could understand. He tried a new tack. "R.C.? Where is he?" He painted a mind's-eye image of the captain, including every physical detail he could recall.

The woman's expression brightened dramatically. She held out her tiny hands, palms upward and said, "R.C." She moved her head in a peculiar angular motion, chin jerking toward her right shoulder. A nod of assent?

Ken beefed up the mental image of the captain he had constructed and replied with his own version of an agreeing nod. "R.C. What have you done with him?"

She frowned and narrowed her black eyes. Then inspiration struck her and she reached out, touching Ken's forehead briefly. As her arm dropped back into her lap, an answering impression filled Ken's mind. Not the clumsy image of Captain Zachary he had created, but the woman's vivid picture of the man. Ken seemed to observe his captain's present activity. He saw Zachary unhurt, in a rock and plastic chamber much like Ken's own. The Survey pilot was exploring his surroundings, stubbornly poking at the unyielding walls.

That was exactly what R.C. would be doing in this situation. It seemed logical, believable. But could Ken believe that what he saw was true? The woman could be putting fantasies into his head, a telepathic placebo to lull rebellion.

Ken remembered one of his courses at the Academy—what to do when captured, what your captors might do. He recalled too many unpleasant options there. One of the less nasty forms of interrogation, though, involved separating two prisoners and letting each man stew on his worry and runaway imagination. It served to break down a captive's resistance. Sometimes the interrogators would put a man off-guard with kindness or let him enjoy the company of a pretty female. But generally, each man would be left alone with his thoughts.

The irony of that warning made Ken laugh. He would never be alone with his thoughts on *this* planet! Briv and his troops could pick a human's brain clean.

"Thayenta." She had spoken aloud, but not in the tone she'd used when they were engaged in a life and death argument in the mist. There was nothing guttural about this word. Her long lashes fluttered over those black eyes and her lips curved upward at the corners.

A smile? Perhaps the aliens didn't smile to indicate friendship. But she was copying Ken's facial expressions, communicating! She touched her breast, duplicating Ken's gesture, and repeated, "Thayenta."

Ken nearly yelped in triumph. He had broken through. He hastily went through the establishing routine he had always thought trite when he saw it on tape dramas. But now it made sense. He pointed to himself and said his name, then at the woman and said, "Thayenta." He repeated the process several times.

He overdid it. Gradually he felt something intruding on this linguistic groundbreaking. Amusement. The woman was laughing at him, telepathically.

"Okay," Ken chuckled, dropping the elaborate gestures and labored enunciations. "So I'm Ken and you're Thayenta. We've got that settled. Thayenta. That's . . ." How could he compliment her on a pretty name? Ken envisioned a flower, mentally calling it "Thayenta."

The woman uttered a tiny sound that was a cross between a sneeze and a giggle. Then he sensed her touching him, mind to mind. A countering image replaced Ken's lumpy picture of a flower. He saw a night scene on an alien world—strange trees and oddly shaped boulders drenched in an eerie lunar light. A beautiful luminescence shifted slowly across that cool, dark landscape as several moons orbited a distant world. The shadow of a tree fell on lush, gray-colored grass. He saw a moon shadow, as fragile and delicate as a fairy carpet.

The loveliness of this visual poetry took Ken aback. He hadn't anticipated stepping directly into the alien culture or its unexpected richness. "Thayenta. I understand," and Ken let himself ride on that night image for a few more seconds. He was embarrassed by his ineptness and inability to use her telepathic language. "I'm afraid my name doesn't mean anything. Or if it does, I don't know what it is."

She moved a few centimeters closer to him, and Ken longed to touch her jewel-like skin once more. A pair of light stabs nudged each side of his throat as a warning. There was no one else in the rock and plastic cell, but he had been told to keep his hands to himself. Was it Briv, reminding Ken that there were other aliens, possibly watching and listening to everything that happened?

Thayenta extended her hands, palms up. And suddenly Ken knew what was wanted of him. Half dreading another painful nudge from Briv, he placed his fingers lightly on Thayenta's, barely making contact. But there was no recurrence of the stabbing sensation. They had read his mind and knew he would behave himself.

Thayenta was struggling to pronounce an unfamiliar Terran word. "Fri . . . end."

Ken's jaw dropped. "Yes! Friend. R.C. and I came here in friendship."

Thayenta closed her eyes briefly, and Kent felt her fingertips caress his lips, gently coaching him to silence. But she hadn't moved! Her fingers were still touching his in that alien handshake.

No, she hadn't touched his lips physically.

Ken's mind reeled. There were so many new experiences and sensations to learn.

She drew back, releasing his hands. But the telepathic contact remained with him, an invisible bond. She cocked her head coyly and a tress of her green-black hair tumbled over her high brow. Tiny veins of rainbow color threaded under her pale skin, transparent ivory shot through with a tracery of bright jewels.

"Can't you tell me where you came from?" he asked gently, trying his damnedest to put his words into thoughts at the same time. "This blurry, misty place—what is it? Do you live here? Did you make the ship crash? And the way the wiring burned—did you do that too? Are you trying to keep us here?"

Thayenta seemed troubled. Perhaps he was going too fast, demanding too much. He felt sympathy and understanding. Although it was not identical to his own, he sensed a reaching out from her alienness to his humanness.

At times she behaved as if she were unsure, walking on thin ice. Was she afraid of being slapped down by Briv? The relationships among the aliens were a puzzle to Ken, but he began to suspect Thayenta's position among her people was low-ranked. Everything she did and thought was being scrutinized.

What would happen if she miscalculated in her job? Would Briv punish her? Would Thayenta receive demerits, like a cadet at the Academy who'd inadvertently broken the rules? Or would the chastisement be telepathic, incomprehensible to humans?

Abruptly, Thayenta stood up and walked toward one of the plastic walls. Ken felt the tug of an invisible leash. She wanted him to follow her, and she was pulling the reins. In Thayenta's telepathic terms, he was certainly a retardate.

Ken obeyed. As he neared the wall it dilated, a white membrane forming an ovate door. There was no need for doorknobs or keys or jailors standing guard. Without telepathy, Ken hadn't a chance to operate the alien locks. It was galling to be utterly dependent on the alien's whims.

He followed Thayenta through the ovate door and stepped into another rock and plastic cell. The door sucked closed behind them, and no evidence of its existence remained.

R.C. stood with his back to Ken and the woman, still prodding at the jointure of the limestone and plastic walls. Refusing to admit defeat, he was looking for a chink.

"Captain," Ken exclaimed, and Zachary spun around. Thayenta dropped the telepathic leash, letting Ken move freely. He started toward the pilot, asking, "Are you all right?" Then he stopped, reading the man's narrow-eyed suspicion.

"How do I know you're really here—or that you're really Ken?" Zachary demanded. His stare shifted to the woman, then back to his apprentice. "You both may be illusions." R.C. waved at the walls. "Maybe those don't exist. Maybe they're images put in my mind to delude me."

Ken realized the possibility. Was what he saw truly Captain Zachary? After a moment Ken lost his skepticism. The aliens couldn't have done such a thorough job. Nobody could imitate that clipped speech and solemn countenance so perfectly. Gradually the tenseness eased out of R.C.'s wiry form as well. His face relaxed a bit. He had weighed similar questions and reached similar conclusions. But his wariness of Thayenta was undiminished. "What's she been doing to you, Ken? Brainwashing you?"

Admittedly R.C. had some experience with telepaths, but Ken trusted his own instincts. "Her name's Thayenta. I've been trying to communicate with her. She called me 'friend'. R.C., I don't think she's an enemy. Remember I told you she tried to talk to me out in space—warn me away from the planet?"

"Warn you off? Why?" R.C. cut away the fat, going to the heart of the problem. "We seem to have crashed in a very convenient location—convenient for the aliens. Right next to the blurry area, their home territory, obviously."

Ken replied unhappily, "I don't have the answer to that yet. We don't have a lot of words in common."

R.C. snorted, unimpressed. "Well, don't let the stars get in your eyes, Ken. We can't count on anything. These aren't mere Capellan Thought-Wings. This is a highly developed telepathic race. That's what we're up against.

"Does it have to be 'up against', Captain?" Ken protested softly. "First contact. It's a great opportunity to establish peaceful relations with these people." Then he paused, remembering. "But maybe we *aren't* their first contact with Terrans. I saw a dead alien; a Terran killed him with a needler."

Morose, R.C. nodded. "Yes, I got the same message, when I first woke up in this cell. I felt a lot of anger riding with it. We're lucky they didn't kill us outright."

"It wasn't luck," Ken countered. "Thayenta was our defense lawyer. It's hard to communicate with her, but in time it will work. Sooner or later she'll explain the significance of this blurry area and why its gravitic effect made us crash."

R.C.'s response shook Ken. The man solemnly wagged his head and said, "Not necessarily. It might have been . . . something else." For a moment he seemed lost in bleak thoughts. Then he looked up and forced a smile at the woman. "Thayenta. That's a pretty name." It was a labored attempt at diplomacy, and it didn't come easily to the gruff space vet.

"She really is trying to help us, Captain," Ken vowed. "We've got to trust her."

"Interesting. If she hadn't shown herself to you out by the shipwreck we might not have fallen into this trap."

Defensively, Ken flared, "Trap? We had already fallen into the trap when we entered this solar system. We didn't have a prayer once that gravity field locked onto us. Once we were down, Briv had control over us. We ought to be grateful to Thayenta for pleading our case."

He hesitated, surprised at his bluntness. His response had bordered on insubordination. But discipline and formality were lax on two-man Survey teams. A rugged, easy-going camaraderie went with the job, which kept a man from going mad for lack of human sociability.

To his relief, R.C. took no offense. "You called him Briv. Good. Now we've got a name to work with. All right, I'll concede at least one point—if the woman hadn't intervened, we might be dead by now."

A series of unwelcome questions persisted in Ken's mind. There were too many mysteries—and not all of them concerning the aliens. Ken checked off the unanswered questions in his mind: a Terran with a needler weapon, a detour to a planet not on the Survey schedule; the diversion R.C. had set up, causing the ship to be in the wrong place at the wrong time. Growing impatience with their predicament forced Ken over the protocol line again. "You never did answer my question, Captain. Why *were* we coming into orbit around NE 592?"

Thayenta was troubled, dismayed by impending conflict between the two Terrans. Ken felt her concern lap his mind, a desire for peace.

Then the wall nearest him melted. There was no mere ovate door this time but a disappearance of the white plastic. It simply ceased to exist.

Ken stared out into a chamber with no discernible boundaries. Horizons vanished into space-black shadows; planes and angles became lost in stygian darkness. In the center was a haven of light, seemingly suspended in a void. A cluster of aliens knelt around a glowing transparent dome, a couple of meters in diameter.

Nine aliens—six males and three females. Thayenta made ten. Was this all of them? If it was an alien colony, it was a damned small one.

Another possibility popped into Ken's mind. Maybe the aliens weren't colonizers but rather an expeditionary force, an advance exploration team for future colonists—as Ken and R.C. were.

"Council," R.C. said, *sotto voce*.

Ken agreed. The aliens formed an inward-facing circle around the glowing dome. Their hands were clenched into fists and resting on their thighs, their eyes squinted. Were they concentrating, putting out telepathic effort?

Thayenta edged close to him and Ken caught a scent that hadn't been there moments before. It was sweetly redolent and very strong. An old phrase seemed appropriate—the scent of fear.

What was the subject of this council? Were they debating the humans' fate? Briv knelt at the far side of the circle, and his countenance wasn't reassuring. That bony face was taut and the dark eyes squinted into nothingness.

Ken put his arm around Thayenta, drawing her close. She was trembling. Was she afraid for herself, or for him? It was comforting to think she cared about what happened to him—an alien, and a member of a species who had apparently murdered one of the jewel-skinned people.

But her concern was probably practical and personal. Briv had knocked her aside during that fracas near the ship. He had silenced her up as though she were an inconsequential nuisance, or an apprentice. That was a situation he could empathize with. In some systems, an apprentice was tightly bound by rules and regulations. Thayenta had broken the rules and presumed above her station, warning the Terrans of danger, and speaking out of turn.

How much had she risked by taking the humans' side? Was it a generous impulse that might cost her dearly? For all Ken knew, her life might be on the line as a result. And her gesture was futile from the first. Once that gravity trap closed on their ship, there was nothing Ken or R.C. could do to avoid crashing on the planet. Thayenta must have assumed human technology was much more formidable than it actually was.

He was being dragged forward: he and R.C. and Thayenta were telepathically hustled into the shadow-framed chamber. Ken scruffed his boots along the uneven plastic floor, resisting, but to little avail. Too much power pulled at him.

Briv got to his feet, and the other aliens turned to face the new arrivals. All wore masks of flesh; absolutely nothing showed in their expressions—neither hatred nor friendship.

Briv walked around the glowing dome, coming toward the humans and Thayenta. He jerked up his left arm and the dome disappeared. In its place stood a concretion of scintillating light, an iridescent blob, unlike the transparent dome.

Ken found himself unable to look at it. It hurt his eyes merely to catch sidelong glimpses of the bright rainbow-colored object. He winced away from a direct stare.

Held in rigid telepathic manacles, Ken was unable to move a muscle. He sensed a terrible tension among the aliens and felt Thayenta's fear as forcefully as if she'd screamed.

Briv plucked at the air again, and some of the unbearable brightness faded from the brilliant blob of color. Ken could see it clearly, though he had to half-shut his eyes. The thing *behaved* like a prism— shattering white light into the spectrum. How it did so, and where the source of the white light lay, Ken couldn't begin to guess. Despite the prismatic function, the object resembled a shapeless lump, its form shifting constantly.

Then Ken saw that Briv was holding a metallic object, a smooth oblong contrivance, roughly ten centimeters long. The alien leader's moss green clothing molded itself to his body, leaving no margin for pockets. Where had Briv gotten the metal object?

Had he plucked it out of the air, perhaps?

That made a crazy kind of sense. Briv had grabbed the air, causing the lumpish prism to lose some of its glitter. The prism must have transmitted the metallic oblong to this chamber from somewhere else. An alien matter transmitter!

But Briv didn't aim the object at the helpless humans. Instead he lifted it toward his throat. The green moss of his clothing changed form, growing a tendril, a mossy cord on which to hang the metal oblong. Ken goggled with admiration. If you need a pocket or an extra sleeve just *think* it into existence. If only humans had such abilities!

Briv spoke. His lips moved, but the words weren't coming from his mouth. They issued from the metallic oblong slung against his chest, and the words were Terran. Inflectionless, mechanical, shimmeringly filtered.

"You will know and we will know many questions and many answers. You are the same as the death-bringers. Then tell us: why do you not deserve death for what you have done to our brother, Hli?"

CHAPTER 6

"A translator!" Ken exclaimed.

"And beautiful miniaturization." R.C. agreed with his usual detachment.

Ken growled, "Why the hell didn't they use that in the first place? Why have we had to flail around like this, trying to guess what they're saying?"

"Wait," the captain warned. "Listen. We've got to dig for every nuance. Don't miss anything."

True. One misinterpreted syllable, and the humans might die.

Loudly, addressing Briv, R.C. said, "We want to know what happened, too. Why do you call us the death-bringers? We brought you no death. We do not even carry weapons."

A risky revelation, but probably necessary to gain the aliens' trust. The aliens didn't look at each other. All of them stared hard at R.C. Ken presumed the translator worked both ways, converting human speech into the aliens' own tongue—or into their thought patterns.

"Death-bringers. *Your* kind," and Briv pointed accusingly at the two Surveymen. A corroborating image rammed into Ken's mind. Thayenta's telepathic pictures were gentle, flowing softly. Briv threw his mental communications like barbed spears.

Ken saw himself, R.C., and a number of other humans. Except for the two Surveymen, the Terrans were indistinguishable, their features vague. The clothes were identical. At first the cookie-cutter sameness of the people puzzled him. Then an old joke cropped up in his mind: "All those aliens look alike to me." Briv lumped all humans together with bigoted disdain.

Then a second telepath intruded into the strange conversation. A softer "voice" fleshed out the unknown humans somewhat. They didn't acquire individuality—as had Ken and R.C. in the images—but they came alive.

Thayenta piped up. An apprentice timidly worming her way into a high-level alien conference, she was speaking out of turn, again.

The telepathic picture broadened. The humans were in a natural setting, moving about in a valley with purplish grass and other flora indigenous to planet NE 592.

"Humans," he said incredulously. "Here. On this world. They've seen other humans right here!"

It didn't make any sense at all. Or did it? The last images Ken had spotted on his mapping screen, just before the ship lost total control up there in space, were of structures of some kind—buildings. "R.C.," Ken said uncertainly. "That doesn't surprise you, does it?"

"We'll talk about it later," the pilot temporized. He concentrated on the immediate problem, talking to Briv. "We did not know these people were on this planet. I assure you, we did not know—"

Invisible claws raked through Ken's brain. Talons of pain and pressure dug into his temples and along the surface of his scalp wound. He felt rather than heard R.C. groan under a similar assault. It was a massive invasion; the telepaths pawed relentlessly through the humans' minds, seeking information.

Battered by pain, Ken dropped to his knees. Thayenta clutched his arm sympathetically, tears spilling from her black eyes. The cruel interrogation raged on, about to crack his skull.

R.C. told them the Surveymen weren't armed. They hadn't drawn first blood. Why were they being subjected to this torture?

But maybe other Terrans had killed one of the aliens. Who was the human with the needler? Since Briv lumped all humans together into the same file and labelled it "Killers," Ken and R.C. had to suffer for that crime.

Fresh pain hit Ken, a deep, emotional wrench that tore a phantom limb from his psychic body. Thayenta was staggering across the vast chamber, her hands out, palms upward in appeal.

Ken forced a cry past his constricted vocal cords. "Thayenta! No!"

Even as he spoke she was driven downward, falling to the floor and writhing. Briv hadn't struck her with his fists. But a telepathic blow was just as potent.

Fury hit Ken in a red flood. Adrenaline charged energy into his shaking body enabling him to move. He half-crawled across the room to the alien woman and knelt beside her.

There was no mark on her, but her pain was real. She sobbed in agony.

Enraged, Ken gathered himself to smash fists into Briv's hard face.

Instantly, the pain in his head was gone, leaving a receding pool of acid dribbling away from his consciousness.

"We see. We know." Briv, using the alien translator, deigning to speak. And for the first time there was a conciliatory expression softening Briv's bony features.

His peacemaking gesture came almost too late. Ken stomped forward, wanting only to avenge the recent telepathic outrages. Against that, Ken was inundated with new, warm emotions. Was it an apology? A definite shift in mood emanated from Briv and the other aliens circled around the bright prism.

"Ken," R.C. appealed. Ken glanced behind him. Thayenta wasn't writhing any more, and the pilot helped her to her feet. R.C. too, released from telepathic bondage, was able to move now.

Another voice added its weight to the captain's. Thayenta held out a hand, supplicating. "Ken . . ." Calmness washed over him, soothing his rage. The combined alien goodwill campaign was effective. Thayenta clinched it with, "Ken, we see," repeating Briv's announcement.

Gradually, Ken's lethal fury melted. But he threw Briv one last glare.

The pleasant, apologetic "vibes" continued unabated. Was it possible Ken had scored a telling point?

R.C. was supporting Thayenta. She still looked a little shaken. And the pilot's face was pale, testimony to the pain he'd endured.

"We had not realized this of you," Briv's translator was relaying. "You Terrans are very different from our kind."

Ken got the distinct impression Briv had almost called them "death-bringers" again, then changed the description. Another concession? Briv didn't appear to be someone who would make many of those.

"What didn't you realize?" R.C. cut in. "That we would fight back, if we could? That we didn't kill one of your people? That we really didn't know there were other humans on this planet?"

Briv's dark gaze shifted calculatingly toward R.C. "You did not know. Yet you came here to look for them."

The remark left the Survey pilot very uncomfortable. It was a temptation, an opening Ken had to resist manfully. He had some questions along exactly those lines himself. But now it was necessary to present a united front, to convince Briv the two humans agreed on everything. Later, when he and R.C. were alone, Ken intended to find out the answers.

But the likelihood of their ever being alone on a

planet they shared with ten telepaths was slim. That was an aspect of human-alien contact that Ken had never considered before this survey.

Briv and Thayenta looked at each other intently. Ken felt a subliminal tingling. Was he picking up more telepathic slopover? He might be a sensitive, with a latent talent for detecting such communications. There was little opportunity to practise the skill among humans.

But the result was a frustrating partial deafness. Ken felt the play of emotions back and forth—stern resolution, tolerance, a desire for satisfaction in some grim matter, and a willingness to compromise. But no details, no specifics came through.

An odd expression reshaped Briv's hard face. He seemed amused, a man listening to a child's humor or a teasing passage of music. Then, abruptly, he plucked the translator off his clothing. The moss green fabric instantly reshaped itself, absorbing the thong it had created. Briv offered the precious metallic oblong to Thayenta.

She didn't smile, but her joy winged its way to Ken, and he read her surprise and pleasure in the heightened color of her skin and the sparkle in her eyes. She raised the translator to her throat, and her pink robes formed a thong suitable for holding the object. He noted wryly that her telepathic dress designing was done with a woman's touch: the translator was suspended from a cord shot through with silvery threads intertwining with the leaflike pink.

The translator reduced language to toneless phonemes, totally impersonal. But Thayenta's words meant something still. "We did not know you would suffer such pain. Real pain. It is because you have no . . . no shields."

Of course. If the telepaths could wield mental weapons against each other, they must have developed self defenses over the millennia. Maybe Thayenta hadn't been in such agony as she'd seemed. The puny humans, on the other hand, were wide open for telepathic attack. Their evolution had taken a different turn; they relied on speech rather than thought transmission.

"He attacked you with the pain, too," Ken accused, glaring at Briv.

"That is another matter," Thayenta said, glancing nervously at the alien leader. Briv was listening closely. It must be an effort for him, this abnormal method of communication. The aliens didn't seem to use speech much at all—except for Thayenta.

R.C. cleared his throat and said loftily, "Then may we assume you apologize for our ill treatment?" Ken envied the pilot's aplomb. The captain spoke as calmly as if they were all seated around a conference table.

Ken felt a bubble of telepathic discussion among the circle of aliens. At last they gave instructions to Thayenta. He was relieved that she was to act as their spokeswoman. She said, "Yes. We *are* sorry for your pain." She gave certain words emphasis by pronouncing them loudly, and the translator duplicated her volume. "That is our way to find truth. But we did not know your minds were so . . . fragile."

Thayenta's statements were broken with awkward

pauses as she sought for precise phrases. Was she afraid she'd make a mistake? Ken knew the feeling. An apprentice is always putting his foot in it. Only during this past year, out from under the Academy's smothering influence, had Ken himself gained polish and confidence, losing his greener mannerisms. Was Thayenta fresh out of an alien Academy, still unsure of herself?

"You look just like the death-bringers," Thayenta explained. "Briv—we assumed you had come to join them, to bring death, as they did."

A little slip of the tongue there? Briv had assumed, and he was the leader. But had *all* of the aliens assumed the Surveymen were "death-bringers"? Thayenta had tried to warn Ken away from the planet, so her motives at least had to be ambiguous.

R.C. spoke to the alien leader. "According to our maps, there are none of our people on this world save ourselves. And according to our maps *you* shouldn't be here, either. We are very curious to know where you came from."

Silence. Thayenta looked timorously at Briv, awaiting instructions.

Briv jerked his head in that alien nod, chin toward his right shoulder. Permission granted, Thayenta went on, "We are the M'Nae. We came here with the Gera-ana. This world is ours. We were here before the death-bringers came."

Ken and R.C. glanced at one another. The pilot spoke for them both. "In what way did you come to this world? *Our* people came to this world twenty orbits ago." Since there wouldn't be any exact correlation for Terran "years," he settled on "orbits" logically. R.C. went on slowly, "Our people explored this world, and there was no one here. Not our people *. . . or* the M'Nae."

Briv tensed and looked sharply at Thayenta, winging an order her way silently. She hastily used the translator again. "It is the world of the M'Nae. We were here before the death-bringers."

"Apparently that's their story and we're stuck with it," Ken muttered. He stared at the prism of shifting shapes, the alien transmitter. What kind of range did it have? Enough to send the M'Nae from one world to another?

But the theory of matter transmitters demanded a reception point—some kind of focussing device—at the terminal.

R.C. sighed, giving up on his original tack, adopting another. "Very well. May we know what happened between you and these death-bringers? You showed us an image of one of the M'Nae lying dead. And you showed us a human with a weapon. How did the death occur? Was there a battle?"

More telepathic conferring. When it was over, Thayenta said, "Hli was our speaker, our dealer with other peoples—should we meet any. When we saw the death-bringers come, Hli went to them to speak with them. He was to tell them that this is our world, and they must leave it to the M'Nae."

"Ambassador from the M'Nae to the Terrans," Ken speculated softly.

"And an ambassador should be secure from attack," R.C. said.

Thayenta licked her pale lips, shivering at the memory of what had happened. "They would not let Hli speak. They came at him with evil. Hli tried to come back to the shadow of the Iontran. But before he could, one of the death-bringers killed him."

Again that bloody image, a recreation of tragedy, erupted in Ken's mind, underlining Thayenta's narration. The effect wasn't dulled by repetition.

"Iontran," he said when the murderous image faded. "The shadow of the Iontran." He wove pieces of the puzzle together. There were still many gaps in it, but the holes were filling up. That prism, the blurred area they'd seen from space, the purple mist; the Iontran could have been any one of those items, or all of them together.

There had been a debate among the M'Nae. Now Briv snatched the translator back from Thayenta rudely, saying, "You are of the same species as the death-bringers. They will not kill you. They will listen to you."

". . . and you want *us* to carry the message this time," R.C. finished for the alien leader.

The "death-bringers" had already killed the M'Nae ambassador in cold blood. What guarantee was there that they wouldn't shoot anyone on sight—human or not?

"Yes! This is M'Nae world. The Gera-ana is now in place. Soon our followers will come. The world must be ready for the M'Nae!"

More of them were coming. That meant more chances for fatal clashes between M'Nae and humans.

Ken pondered the crux of the matter. Who were

those other humans, the death-bringers? "A ship-wreck," he said, the logic inescapable. The captain didn't respond. Ken pursued the point. "If some humans crashed here, maybe they were dragged down by that same gravity force. And maybe they've got a working sub-space radio left. But if that's true, why haven't they sent out an S.O.S.?"

"Perhaps they did, and Earth Central hasn't received it yet." R.C. said. 'We're a long ways out."

"Not that far out," Ken argued, unconvinced. R.C. let it lie. The variables stretched in all directions. "There's only one way we're going to get to the bottom of this. Take the M'Nae up on it. We'll have to go and talk with these 'death-bringers'."

"If we can get to them without being killed," R.C. reminded him. "At least the M'Nae are willing to let us try."

Zachary turned to Briv and said formally, "We will present the M'Nae claim to these other humans. But how shall we go to them? We don't know where we are. You have captured us and brought us to this place in the mist. Our ship has been destroyed, and all our equipment. . . ."

Destroyed by telepathic overload? Ken wondered. If Briv could bring him and the captain to the ground with those telepathic claws and materialize objects out of nothing, he could probably burn the sup-posedly non-flammable, non-explosive wiring inside a ship's bulkheads.

Briv stabbed a finger at Thayenta. "She will go with you."

Thayenta jumped. Apparently that physical reaction was the same for both M'Nae and humans. Ken put himself in her shoes—ordered to volunteer for a very dangerous mission. The last M'Nae who'd ventured into the territory of these unknown humans had ended up dead.

R.C. wasn't pleased by the assignment. "That won't be necessary. If you'll just show us the way, we will arrange to meet the Terrans ourselves."

"She will go with you," Briv said with heavy finality. This decision wasn't for the humans' convenience, but for the M'Nae. "She is now our speaker, our dealer with other peoples. She will find for us the death-bringer who killed Hli."

As a result of his ambassador's death, Briv was short a subordinate so he would appoint a new ambassador: An apprentice who liked to talk too much and lowered herself to the point of associating with humans. There was a tinge of sadism in Briv's order.

He was sending R.C. and Ken out as Judas goats, and Thayenta along as a spy and a cheap sacrifice, if required. They must go to the humans who had killed the first ambassador, pinpoint the murderer, and then deliver the man to the M'Nae.

Ken had gone through an exquisitely painful sample of Briv's punishment technique—a simple search for information. What would Briv do to the man who had killed his ambassador? Maybe the human had panicked, seeing an alien on this supposedly uninhabited world.

"We'll have to accept," R.C. whispered, unhappy at the prospect.

"Captain, if the woman is going with us, I can

work with her," Ken said encouragingly. "She's not vindictive. There will be some cooperation going both ways."

"Maybe you can reach her, Ken, but so can Briv," R.C. said. "However, we have no choice."

THE alien leader returned the translator to Thayenta. It seemed to constitute the only supplies she was going to get on her hazardous assignment. Briv eyed the translator with disgust, glad to be rid of it. In his view, it was merely a device to cope with an inferior, non-telepathic race, not a useful tool.

Thayenta pulled her shoulders back and held her head high, silently acknowledging her orders and receipt of the translator. Then she walked toward Ken and R.C. She looked apprehensive, a young woman tackling a large job, one she feared was too big for her.

Without farewell to her people, Thayenta started walking into the shadows of the prism-room. Ken and R.C. followed her uncertainly. Were they on their way to the "death-bringers" right now?

A few strides farther, the great open space containing the prism and the alien conference disappeared, swallowed up in the darkness. Ahead of Thayenta a ribbon of light stretched out, simultaneously lengthening on their pathway and shrinking to the rear. An alien spotlight tracked them as they walked. Ken matched Thayenta's pace, staying within that nimbus. He craned his neck, trying to discern the source of the mysterious light. No originating point was apparent—not to the side, front, rear, or overhead.

The ribbon of light simply was a path leading them into nowhere.

Thayenta took the endless stretching and shrinking sourceless light for granted. It was part of her world and no more in need of explanation than her clothing made from willow leaves, the glowing, constantly shape-changing prism-transmitter, the plastic that wasn't plastic lining the walls of their dungeons, or the doors that appeared and disappeared without use of machinery.

Ken accepted many things from his own culture without inquiry. He couldn't build a spaceship or refine metal or manufacture the cloth that made up his fatigues, but he didn't puzzle over such matters, either. He accepted them and used them.

A little farther on, she held up her hand and the light-path suddenly stopped. In the same instant the world expanded as though illusionary curtains were being drawn back. A flood of natural light fell over the three travellers, and the purplish mist was all around them.

A stream rippled by, half a meter away. R.C. squatted on the bank and stirred some floating twigs. "Water," he said, a bit disappointed. "Plain, everyday water." He fingered the grass on the side of the stream. Typical flora of NE 592. "I think we're back in real time and space again."

Thayenta sidled past Ken and R.C., heading for a white, irregularly formed raft of Briv's plastic wedged onto the bank of the fog-swathed stream. Thayenta stepped out onto it, then looked back at the men, puzzled by their hesitation. "Please step onto the carrier. We must travel thirty jarda-ans before we reach your people."

"Terrans," Ken defined for her. Warily, he planted a boot on the plastic raft, then hurriedly shifted his full weight on board. The craft teetered a bit, then stabilized. It wobbled again as R.C. jumped onto it, then settled onto the stream's current.

The current was sluggish, but they made good progress. Thayenta was narrow-eyed, concentrating, tuning up some alien power for the plastic raft. In a few seconds they were sailing along at a speedy clip.

Although the raft rode smoothly, Ken would have preferred a more sedate ride. He presumed Thayenta knew what she was doing, but it gave him a queasy feeling to be floating so quickly on an uncharted stream without any conception of his destination.

CHAPTER 7

R.C. was watching Thayenta. She stood near the bow of the alien raft, gazing ahead into the mist and concentrating very hard on her telepathic powering and steering of the wavy sheet of plastic. Since her back was to the men, Ken had no difficulty guessing what was on R.C.'s mind.

"I don't believe that's a good idea, Captain," he said politely. "I'm not sure you should even think it. Briv is probably eavesdropping, tuning in on everything."

"Oh?" R.C. was deceptively blank. "Just what idea were you talking about?"

"Grabbing Thayenta as a hostage." As Ken spoke her name the woman turned to look at them briefly. If she understood the discussion, she gave no sign of it. She devoted her attention to steering the raft.

"It seemed a viable tactic," R.C. muttered, conceding Ken's guess.

"They'd never let us get away with such a hostile gesture." Ken sat down, determined to enjoy the raft cruise as long as it might last.

R.C. sighed and slumped down beside his apprentice. The pilot massaged his eyelids. "Telepaths. That covers a multitude of possibilities. There are so many theories, and we have very little experience with true races of the creatures."

"You've dealt with the Capellan Thought-Wings," Ken began.

Sloughing past experience aside, R.C. said, "That doesn't apply at all. It's completely new territory." The older man sighed again and smiled wanly. "All the telepathic species I've encountered were primitive types. The Capellans are practically embryos compared to Briv and Thayenta and the others. No, the two of us are starting fresh. Nothing I've dealt with can help us here on NE 592, not with the M'Nae."

The Survey pilot traced an invisible figure one on the raft's irregular surface. "One telepathic ability we've confirmed. They can force themselves into our minds."

"But how much did they learn when they did?" Ken argued. "Until Briv teleported that translator to the conference, we were operating on totally different wavelengths. Language alone is a terrific barrier. You said it yourself—we had to catch every nuance. So do they."

"Agreed. They may not know much more about us than we do about them." R.C. traced a two beside the invisible one. "All right. We've learned they can teleport objects, range and size limitations unknown to us as yet. Three—they've got that undulative machine with the prismatic effect."

"Their matter transmitter terminal," Ken offered. R.C. mulled that over for a moment, then nodded.

"How did they get it here?" the older man asked. "I didn't see any indications of a space ship technology."

"Or any other technology, as we know technology," Ken said. "We have to assume they teleported the prism here from—"

"Another planet." R.C. and Ken stared at each other, and the pilot cracked out a rare, incredulous grin. "If that's an explanation, the whole thing's beyond our comprehension."

Ken leaned forward and spoke earnestly. "Maybe we're beyond theirs, Captain. Thayenta projected her image out to me in space, warning us to get away before we were trapped in their gravity field. She really believed we could pull away. Suppose the M'Nae don't realize what Terran technology can— and can't—do, how limited we are."

"Very limited," R.C. agreed sourly. "As far as we're concerned, it might as well be non-existent."

"Unless these 'death-bringers' salvaged some equipment from *their* shipwreck," Ken said. "I wonder what kind of equipment it could be? Civilian, or military? The needlers the M'Nae showed us in the telepathic images are definitely Patrol weapons. But wouldn't we have heard about a Patrol ship missing in this vicinity?"

After a year as Zachary's apprentice, Ken had learned to detect the subtle shifts and alterations in the man's seemingly inscrutable face. What Ken read now made him press for an answer. "You know who these Terrans are, don't you?"

There was a long silence. Thayenta drove the raft

swiftly down the stream. Along the banks indigenous fauna—insects, birds thrumming songs, skittering rodents—rustled and hopped in the purplish grass and pink-leaved willows. They rode through a foggy Eden. Not a harsh world, a man could get used to it, if he must.

"Captain," Ken prodded gently, "I'll have to know sometime. We're on our way to meet with these Terrans right now. Do I have to play junior ambassador when I don't know what my government's instructions are?"

His feeble joke did the trick. R.C. evaded Ken's gaze as he said, "I didn't want to keep you in the dark. Orders."

It fitted. R.C. Zachary, the by-the-book expert. He'd take such orders from HQ, even if he didn't like them. Ken let the pilot off the hook. "There isn't much point in top secrets now. HQ won't hear from us for months, unless they automatically track you down. Were the orders critical to security?"

R.C. shook his head, retracing the series of numerals he had drawn on the raft. "Not critical. And I'm afraid in some respects I made sure we'd be hard to find—not specifying to HQ exactly which nooks and crannies I'd take, or in what order." Ken gawked, hardly able to accept such deviant behavior, and the space veteran looked embarrassed. "I didn't expect things to end up *this* way, but when I took the assignment I never dreamed we'd run smack into the M'Nae."

Ken sucked in a deep breath of the foggy air. "Now that we're here, what's the score?"

"Postulate a gap in the master ship inventory at Earth Central Clearing. The computer runs a standard, random check and comes up short one old mercantile hauler, a Class-D. It should have been safely mothballed in the Proxima asteroids. But it wasn't." Some of R.C.'s outrage at the theft was betrayed in his tone.

Ken whistled, earning a glance from Thayenta. He smiled at her, and she turned back to her steering, apparently reassured that whistling wasn't a Terran alarm. Lowering his voice, Ken said, "Stealing a Class-D would take a lot of courage and planning. You can't just walk out of a deep-spacer berth with a ship under your arm. It would take a crew, fuel—"

"And connections," R.C. added, his furry brows drawn. "Bribery in high places and manipulation of the computer inventory. The theft would have gone unnoticed for years if a random check hadn't caught it. One missing ship, fuel illegally requisitioned—"

"Let me guess," Ken interrupted. "A five-year food supply, building materials, medicines—the manifest you would have for a Pioneer Colony." R.C. brightened appreciatively, gesturing for Ken to continue. "It follows the pattern. If you steal a ship and set about hiding the evidence for years, that means one of two things. Either you're ready to start a war, or you're planning to get a long way off the beaten path and hide out on the fringes where the Patrol can't find you."

R.C. slapped a hand down loudly on Ken's shoulder. Thayenta jerked around apprehensively, but her tension melted when she saw the captain's broad smile. Very female, she sniffed disdainfully at these rough, physical habits.

"Good!" the pilot exclaimed.

That one word meant a lot from a man stingy with praise. But Ken kept to the point. "Do you know who engineered this scheme? You said you had several possible starting shots in the investigation. What made you pick NE 592 as a hide-out planet?"

The captain grew introspective. "It had promise. NE 592 was damned far out. The patrol wouldn't come here for decades. But I hadn't counted on that blurry area, or the M'Nae gravity trap."

Again, the pilot was evading a direct answer. Who plotted the spaceship theft?

The purplish mist was thinning rapidly. They must be passing the outer perimeter of M'Nae territory and re-entering the real world of NE 592. The land here was hilly and rocky. The stream's current was picking up as they raced between low banks and boulder outcroppings. A plume of white mist rose up in the distance, and Ken heard a rumble rising to a crescendo.

"Rapids," he speculated worriedly.

Thayenta twisted, facing the right bank of the stream. Her posture was rigid, her eyes narrowed as she bore down on telepathic steering procedures. The raft floated to the right, heading for safe, quiet waters, but ever so slowly.

As one, R.C. and Ken gauged the depth and current of the stream. Not trusting Thayenta to defeat the rapids ahead, the two men jumped off the raft.

The water came up to their knees, and wasn't as

cold as Ken had expected. He and the pilot seized the raft on either side, hand steering it toward the bank.

With a startled squeal, Thayenta sat down in an ungraceful sprawl. Outraged, she gathered herself, straightening a rumpled pink sleeve and her leafy tunic skirt. "Not necessary!" she complained, petulant. "Not necessary. I am in control of the raft."

"We just want to guarantee its safety," explained Ken.

The alien woman clutched the edge of the raft as the men guided it toward a backwater. While she'd been completely confident using telepathic skills, she obviously didn't trust the humans' muscle power. Fair enough, Ken thought, suppressing a laugh; he didn't entirely trust telepathy to keep them from smashing into the rocks.

The raft beached among a stand of blue reeds, overhung with more of the ubiquitous pink willows. Ken clambered up onto the bank, and as Thayenta stood up, he held her about the waist and swung her onto dry land. She was still piqued. "You did not need to do that. . . ." Then she closed a hand over the translator, muffling its operation. A torrent of the M'Nae language battered at the men's ears, none of it seemingly complimentary.

Ken grinned. "Telepath or not, I recognize a woman scorned. R.C., I think we hurt her feelings."

"We might have kept drier if we'd let her do the driving," the pilot admitted, brushing broken reeds off his fatigue pants and boots. "But I'm just as happy we did things our way, for a change."

It was a blunt reminder of recent events, when Ken and R.C. had been puppets at the mercy of the M'Nae. Yes, it had been satisfying to wrestle the raft to shore by their own, non-telepathic, powers.

At first Thayenta refused to be mollified. But finally her black eyes lost their snappish glare. Shyly, she touched fingertips with Ken. She seemed startled when he clasped her hand firmly, human fashion.

"We've been moving southwest," R.C. decided, squinting at NE 592's star.

Ken looked back at the purplish mist. "We crashed at one side of that blurry area and maybe came out the other. That's about fifty kilometers."

"Part of which constitutes 'thirty jarda-ans'," R.C. added.

Thayenta pointed along the bank, downstream. "That way," she said in Terran, without using the translator.

"She's really bright, R.C.," Ken commented. "Thayenta obviously has a gift for languages. The 'death-bringers' are directly downstream. I would ask how far, but we would probably get the answer in 'jarda-ans'," he added ruefully.

Thayenta pursed her lips and resorted to the translator, reluctantly. "The death-bringers are many, and they move about." Then Ken felt a peculiar sensation —someone was tiptoeing through his brain. There was no resemblance to the telepathic assault Briv had flung at the Surveymen. Whatever Thayenta was hunting for, she gave up. The mental probing stopped, and she spoke again in Terran. "Afraid."

Concerned, Ken said, "Afraid of what? Things will be different now. We're with you. We'll straighten this out. It won't be like it was when your first ambassador met them."

He was offering a lot more than he should, making guarantees he had little power to carry out. But Thayenta's fear was genuine, and Ken wanted very much to reassure her.

"They probably have guards posted," R.C. remarked, and Ken agreed, eyeing Thayenta for confirmation.

She made a valiant effort to imitate a human nod, not jerking her head sideways in the M'Nae style but bringing her chin straight down. "Near the place where the death-bringers sleep."

"A village," Ken speculated. "I think I saw one from space, just before we lost our sensors."

"Did you?" R.C. lifted an eyebrow. "They've been busy, haven't they? A village. All right. Thayenta, give us plenty of warning when we get close to any outposts. We don't want to stumble into them blindly."

They followed Thayenta along the banks, heading downstream. There was no path but enough beaten and bare patches surfaced amid the grass to give them easy walking. Ken spent one thoughtful look on the beached raft before it was left behind. Could Thayenta power it upstream? He liked having a means of escape handy.

Quickly memorizing landmarks, Ken tried to frame the question for Thayenta. "Could you propel that raft back where we came from? I mean, can you move things with your mind—like you opened the door to my cell?"

"Not . . . not," and she was forced to resort to the translator again. "Not as adept as Briv."

An apprentice. She'd made a big admission, conceding her own weakness. Ken remembered that he had never caught Thayenta engaging in teleportation.

She sensed his thoughts before he expressed them, and revealed a bit more of herself. "I am kuu-a— student. From the Yen people. We do not move things. I am—" and Thayenta disgustedly clapped her hand over the translator again. "I am speaker."

"A linguist," Ken guessed, elated. "That explains why she's learning Terran so fast."

"Not fast enough," R.C. groused. "It's like pulling teeth to get solid facts."

"We don't want to get her into trouble with her own people," Ken said sharply. "If I was in enemy custody and they were pumping me, you'd be very displeased if I told anyone anything."

"Right," R.C. said ominously.

"She's doing her best to cooperate without betraying the M'Nae," Ken insisted.

"I see that. But *you* have to see something, Ken," and the pilot spoke very seriously. "This could be a full-scale war—"

Five men leapt out from behind boulders and trees, launching themselves at the three travellers.

They shouted wordlessly, faces contorted, and charged like screaming savages, brandishing clubs.

Ken thrust Thayenta behind him and threw up an arm to fend off a cudgel blow. He got hit high and low by two men, but they didn't use their clubs. Instead they tackled him, bowling him back and over on the purplish grass.

Ken defended himself desperately, slamming a fist into one man's face, gaining himself a few centimeters to wriggle.

"Quit it, you stupid bastard!" one man protested. "Get her! Quick!"

Ken wrestled with the thug clutching his legs, and the second man jumped at Thayenta.

"Don't!" Ken roared. "You kill her and you're dead."

His threat had some effect. The man had started to swing the club at Thayenta. During his mid-air pause, she shrieked and stumbled through the grass, running from him.

It was no contest. In a couple of strides, the club wielder cut off Thayenta's escape easily. But this time he swung a fist instead of the club.

Thayenta's black eyes rolled and she crumpled into a pitiful heap at her attacker's feet.

Enraged, Ken flailed free of his attacker and rushed furiously at the man who had struck down Thayenta.

He didn't make it. Both men dived on him, and a third added his weight. Ken was solid and in good condition, but numbers told. Seething with frustration and fury, he wheeled and struggled, but the situation was hopeless.

R.C., a lightweight and carrying twenty-five extra years, was held immobile by the other two thugs. The pilot looked as helpless and angered as Ken.

They were ambushed! They had been snared like raw recruits.

Why hadn't Thayenta warned them?

Ken stared anxiously at the woman. She was breathing, but unconscious. A dark swelling had started on that jewel-skin, just under her right eye.

"Why the hell did you hit her?" Ken shouted. "She isn't armed. What are you cretins using for brains?"

"Ken." R.C. threw him a veiled warning, shutting off Ken's tirade.

Barely in control of his temper, Ken said levelly, "She's an ambassador. You might have treated her like one."

"Ambassador?" and one of the thugs guffawed crudely. But the others began having second thoughts.

"The Chief'll take care of it," they decided, relieved to turn the whole matter over to an authority they plainly respected. "Come on. Let's get movin' before any more o' those things show."

"You're not going to leave her here," Ken said menacingly. He was in no position to enforce his demand, but he put enough cold anger into his voice to win his case.

The club wielders looked at each other uncertainly. "Okay. We'd better take her along."

One man turned spokesman, weakly apologizing to Ken and R.C. "We wasn't sure you guys was Terrans. Sorry for the rough stuff. Don't worry about the female. She ain't hurt bad. Look, we'll take you to see our Chief. He'll get this straightened out."

"Agreed," R.C. said in a cool tone. He and Ken shook off restraining hands and Ken hurried over to Thayenta, feeling her pulse. R.C. added, "Only on condition the woman's not mistreated further. Get that clear right now."

They should have laughed at him. The Surveymen were weaponless and outnumbered. But R.C. Zachary had earned his reputation. That voice of command had been polished for years. The ambushers conferred among themselves, more and more unsure of their ground. They finally nodded, and one of them came to Thayenta, starting to grab her ankles.

Ken knocked the man aside. "Keep your hands off her. You've done enough damage." He gathered the woman in his arms and stood up.

After a momentary hesitation, their captors herded them downstream along the same unmarked path the trio had been following minutes earlier.

Ken glanced at Thayenta. What did variations in alien coloring indicate? He couldn't tell if she was badly hurt or just stunned. Judging by human standards, her pulse had felt light and rapid, but perhaps it was normal for a M'Nae. The lump on Thayenta's cheek had already ripened into an ugly bruise, and Ken vowed that it would be repaid, with interest.

For now, there was nothing to do but shuffle along in R.C.'s wake; one club wielder walked ahead, two flanked the captives, and two more brought up the rear. There was no chance to make a break for it.

Thayenta was very light, probably much less than fifty kilos. He wouldn't tire easily, carrying her. But Ken had a more urgent reason for hoping they reached their destination quickly—there might be medical aid there for Thayenta.

Ken wondered if the men were indicative of the settlement as a whole. If so, no wonder the initial clash between humans and M'Nae had occurred.

Again he wondered why Thayenta hadn't warned them of the ambush. R.C. had specifically asked her to give them plenty of time, yet they'd been caught completely off-guard.

The answer came to him in a flash of intuition. Brute reactions. Briv let go of those telepathic claws when Ken had gone after him in unthinking rage. Possibly the M'Nae could cope with human minds only on a certain level. When a man descended to a savage state, or was too stupid to think deeply like these club wielders, the M'Nae's telepathic abilities were hobbled.

Thayenta was not able to teleport herself. There were a lot of different abilities among the M'Nae, and Ken had no means of discerning what they were and what range they had.

What about Briv? Was he telepathically watching them right now? Wouldn't he have stopped this attack—communicated a warning to Thayenta—if he could have? Ken thought of Briv's bony face and unforgiving manner. How could he guess what motivated the M'Nae leader? Briv wasn't operating on human moral standards. For all Ken could tell, Briv might be using Thayenta and the Surveymen as guinea pigs—throwing them to the "death-bringers" to see what would happen.

The captives and their escort wended their way around a clump of pink and purple foliage that jogged away from some rapids. The rapids broadened and danced downhill toward spectacular falls.

Suddenly a man stepped out of a hiding place amid the willows and approached the group. "What you doing off-station? The Chief told you to—"

"We got something for him." The lead club wielder pointed to Ken, R.C., and Thayenta. "A real prize. Better tell him."

"Right. He's over at this side of the valley, anyway, checking on the water wheel." The trail guard plucked at his belt and Ken stared in shock. The man was using a small personal communicator: standard government issue.

Stolen from a government warehouse? Was it part of a large quantity of supplies to stock a stolen Class-D space ship?

As their captors urged them farther along the trail, the man at the way post spoke urgently into the communicator, notifying someone ahead of their approach.

THE vegetation thinned and the trees stood farther apart now. Ken got a clear view as they came to a turn in the trail, out over a grassy valley nestled between two hill ranges. He momentarily came to a stop, gawking.

His glimpse from space had been right on target. A half-completed colony settlement was in the process of being born. Dwellings and barns and sheds stood surrounded by fields where men and women sweated with primitive farm tools, planting crops.

One of the guards tried to hurry Ken forward. He excused his stop by lifting Thayenta slightly in his arms to get a better grip on her slender body. It gave him a few more seconds to peruse the scene below.

Except for the crude tools and the nature of the log buildings, this could have been any pioneer colony. If things had gone on schedule, sometime ten years in the future, a Second Survey would have approved this world for colonization.

But it was here now. Snugly enclosed in the valley, her people were busily hacking out their future: an agricultural Eden.

The price had come high. There was a scar on Eden's face. A deep gouge traversed the valley's length, paralleling the creek that supplied the village. The gouge shot out the far end of the valley, on to the horizon and out of sight. Ken guessed that it was an entry gouge, left by a Class-D spaceship scraping an abrasion across the planet's skin. The two-man Survey ship had left a similar, smaller scratch on NE 592. A Class-D could swallow the Survey ship whole. Ken could make a visual estimate of that, because the huge interstellar craft had come to rest against the valley's back wall, her nose rammed halfway up to the crest.

"Move along, now," and a club nudged Ken's shoulder.

Ken growled an oath and Thayenta stirred, moaning softly, before lapsing back into unconsciousness. As Ken started forward, the man leading them shouted, "Hold it! Here comes The Chief."

A lanky figure, climbing a footpath beside the falls, hurried past a wooden water wheel and an earthen dam.

R.C. watched the man's approach narrowly. The pilot seemed as unfriendly as Briv, contemplating the advance of a human enemy. Such undisguised animosity from the veteran pilot startled Ken. R.C.'s emotions were showing badly, and he bore no resemblance to an "ambassador."

Ken looked around, hoping the club wielders might be relaxing their guard. They were, but that wasn't much comfort. They were situated on one narrow, completely blocked trail. Three-meters-high boulders were on Ken's right, and a waterfall fell to the left. Chances for an escape attempt were poor, to say the least. And right now the pilot's full attention was directed toward the man coming to meet them.

"Chief, we caught these—" the spokesman for the club wielders began proudly.

"Yes, yes. Good work. Larribee relayed the message," the "Chief" replied, shutting off the braggart's report. The man paused at the top of the waterfall path, staring curiously at R.C. and Ken and Thayenta.

As tall and fierce-looking as Briv, he was scarcely even winded after that climb. The face, the physique, the posture all were achingly familiar to Ken, though he was positive he had never met this man in his life. Perhaps it was the clothes—standard issue military fatigues with the communicator and needler the man wore at his belt. Illegal supplies, to match an illegal colony.

Ken couldn't quite put his finger on a name, but he had seen the face many times. Acne scars pitted a craggy jawline; protruberant eyes flanked a beak of a nose. He had a lion's share of kinky, graying hair. This man's parents had belonged to an old school; they hadn't believed in genetic engineering to ensure physical attractiveness. The man was every centimeter their inheritor.

"R.C.?" The Chief's voice was strained with disbelief. "Is it really you, R.C.?"

Zachary and his apprentice were at a disadvantage, but R.C.'s manner put them on equal ground with their captors. Zachary squared his shoulders and used that commanding tone to perfection. Ken could almost touch the man's contempt. "Yes, it's me. Did you think we wouldn't find you, Noland?"

Everything fell into place. In the pictures and solidopic images Ken had seen, the Chief's face held the look of an eagle—as had R.C. Zachary's portrait twenty-five years ago. Those two men were contemporaries. Members of the Academy's first class, they'd shared an unquenchable drive to reach for the stars. They were men who had pioneered Earth's leap out into the galaxy.

Since Ken was a boy, Noland Eads had been one of his idols. It was an honored name, emblazoned on plaques, prominently featured in textbooks and learning tapes, identified along with R.C.'s in Earth Central's "Outward Bound" Pioneer Hall.

Meeting this hero wasn't at all what Ken had expected.

CHAPTER 8

A jovial grin split Eads' homely face as he slapped R.C.'s biceps. "I'll be damned! It *is* you, R.C.! It must be . . . what? Five years? You haven't changed a bit, you old curmudgeon," and he playfully prodded the shorter man's ribs.

Carefully, not attracting undue attention, Ken knelt, supporting Thayenta's tiny frame across his knees, propping her against his chest. She was a featherweight, but he'd better conserve as much energy as possible. There was no telling when he'd need it in a hurry.

Zachary wasn't lulled by the effusive greeting. "Noland, I said how—"

The hero of Survey brushed away verbal flies. "Oh, let that be. Belongs in the past, R.C. Dead and buried. The important thing is, you're here! What brings you boys out this far? Secondary Survey, huh? Is this your apprentice?"

"Ken Farrell," R.C. said flatly. "He doesn't need to be told who you are."

"Hello there, Ken!" Eads' big hand went out and, mesmerized, Ken responded. Calluses scraped his palm. This was a man who fought nature as he'd fought space. Eads smiled down at him paternally. "You've got a good captain, son. But you know that. Back in the old days, R.C. and I broke new ground many a time. Back when it really *was* a frontier, before it got so damned soft. Right, R.C.? Pity you weren't around then, son. You'd have liked it!"

Three men clambered up the trail and spread out behind Eads. They stood at parade rest, strung along the hill crest between the waterfall and the boulders, effectively blocking any escape attempt in that direction. When these men arrived, Ken noted a shift in manner in the club wielders. On their mettle now that the elite guard was on the scene, they made a half-hearted effort to look military.

The reinforcements were the Praetorians, Noland Eads' special troops. Compared to the thugs, the three men looked professional and alert, their needlers on their belts. Obviously Eads didn't trust anyone but his Praetorians with them.

Thugs and Praetorians all attended Eads with worshipful respect. Ken didn't blame them. He'd long been in awe of Eads himself. The man had that particular presence of command. Even on tape he had looked the hero, the space frontiersman in every way.

Eads glanced at Thayenta in amazement. "You got one of them, and alive! A female. That's great, R.C. How you'd pull it off?"

R.C. stepped in before Ken could antagonize their captors. "We were lost out in that purple muck. The woman helped us. I believe she's lost from her people too, perhaps an outcast. She's harmless."

"Harmless?" Eads' bushy gray eyebrows rose toward his hairline. "She's an alien; this planet's lousy with them, R.C. We didn't even know they were here till one of them came out of that purple mist. There's some kind of gravitic force inside that damned stuff." He glared upstream, toward Briv's territory.

"Deviation," and R.C. flicked a significant warning look at Ken, demanding silence. "Yes, that would explain things. We were coming into orbit when everything on board went haywire."

"Yes, yes!" Frenzy shook Noland Eads. "I tell you, the aliens did it. They made us crash. We don't know what they've got inside there. We can't get at them." Eads lowered his voice and spoke confidentially. "I think they're telepaths, R.C. The first one came out of that stuff wouldn't even talk. Can you imagine it? He sort of projected pictures at us. Pictures! A telepath. Why, he could have picked our brains. No telling what else."

He was whispering in a ludicrous attempt to avoid telepathic eavesdropping. Ken started to smile. Then he realized Eads was serious. He actually thought he could block out the M'Nae with such simple tactics.

"You said the first one," R.C. probed. "You saw others?"

Eads nodded vigorously. "They popped out of nowhere, and then disappeared just like that! I tell you, it was scary as all hell, R.C."

Ken frowned. Eads hadn't told them everything by a long shot. He'd neglected to mention *why* the aliens had "popped out of nowhere." They had been teleporting out of M'Nae territory to rescue the body of their murdered ambassador, killed by Eads or one of his men.

"I don't think the girl's in that class," R.C. said, offhand, as though bored with the subject. "If she's a telepath, she's a very low-level one. And she talks—particularly to my apprentice." He winked elaborately at Eads and finished, "the only image she projects is that she's got stars in her eyes. You know how kids are."

Surreptitiously, Ken fumbled at the pink and silver cord circling Thayenta's throat. He feared it would resist, but the alien translator popped loose after a slight tug. Ken slid the metal oblong into a slit pocket on the thigh of his fatigues. Eads mustn't see the device. Not while so many questions remained unanswered, and more cropped up every minute.

"They're dangerous," Eads argued loudly, smacking a fist into a callused palm. "They're responsible for that gravity field in there. They made us crash."

With a show of grudging agreement, Zachary nodded.

"Hah! I was sure of it. Admit it. It didn't make any difference how much retro pack you pulled, did it?" Eads crowed in bitter triumph. "Once that alien field got hold of you, down you went."

"I couldn't break it," R.C. conceded. "We were lucky to get out of that crash alive."

"Yes, yes! Lucky. It's fate, that's what it is, R.C. We were meant to be here—both of us," Eads said with startling enthusiasm.

Fate? Ken eyed the huge cargo ship wedged against the valley's back wall. Not fate but a damned good pilot got that ship down. Like the Survey ship the cargo vessel had strewn her guts all along that gouge she had carved across the planet's surface. Buckled plates and great rips in the Class-D's hull testified to impact force. Ken doubted that everyone on board had lived through the crash. It was a miracle so many people were now able to work the farm fields and build the huts in the valley—and stand guard for Noland Eads.

"I thought she'd finished me a couple of times," and Eads became somber for a few moments. "Cost us eighteen good people, R.C., that crash." Then he thrust that behind him, talking too fast as he relived the crisis. "Pulled the emergency package and every auxiliary, the lifeboats, you name it, R.C. I pulled it. The whole damned rig, but I got her down. I was *meant* to. Fate meant for us to cheat those aliens, show them we could take everything they'd dish out."

He was the model of a space veteran, zooming hands in the air to describe maneuvers, imitating the ship's harrowing slide in. But Eads' color was very high, a stammer tripping his tongue now and then, his eyes glittering.

R.C. darted a glance at Ken, then said, "We went through the same business on a smaller scale. Looks like you hit easier than we did, Noland. There's nothing left of our ship but junk. Even communications are gone."

He put a slight emphasis on that last sentence, and Eads caught the import. He relaxed visibly—obviously delighted to hear that no Mayday had gone out from the Survey ship. It seemed Eads did not want

Earth Central to discover that there were two ships and dozens of humans down on NE 592 with no hope of escape without outside help.

Why would any sane man want to be marooned for months—maybe years—alone in a vast universe?

Any *sane* man. Did Noland Eads fit that description? By Ken's standards the man wasn't acting rationally. He had stolen a ship, supplies, and outlawed weapons; he had initiated a colony on a planet without any authorization. And Eads was revelling in the announcement that Zachary had not been able to send an S.O.S.

He didn't *want* to be found.

Thayenta moved, whimpering, fumbling for the bruise on her cheek. Ken gently caught her hand and prevented that. As he restrained her Eads cried, "She mustn't wake up. She'll destroy us! She'll call the rest of those aliens!"

Protectively, Ken hovered over the woman. "She won't give you any trouble," he retorted. Then he recalled R.C.'s "cover story." Belligerence was the wrong tack. Ken altered his manner, played it callow, though it galled him. "I'll take care of her. She's okay. Honest."

Was he laying it on too thick? He had to play the young fool just right and turn Eads' wrath aside. Eads' anger shifted momentarily toward Ken, then softened into a Dutch-uncle smile. "Believe me, son, she's dangerous. Oh, maybe not the girl. But you don't see all the possibilities. There are more of them, and they're telepaths. They'll pick your brains just like vultures!"

Eads spoke more accurately than he realized. Briv indeed had telepathic vulture's claws, and knew how to use them.

Past Eads' shoulder, Ken saw R.C. nod approval of his naive, love-struck act. Ken swallowed his pride and pursued that line. "I'll vouch for her, sir. I promise she won't give you any trouble. Will you, honey?"

Ken thought hard, desperately sending a warning to the alien woman, praying she'd get the message. Thayenta stared up into Eads' rugged face and flinched back against Ken. *No,* Ken beamed at her. *Don't panic. Play it timid but harmless.* She must convince Eads she was both.

Above all Briv and his troops must not teleport out of the mist and try to rescue Thayenta. The situation was too tense; there were too many needlers. Any clash would result in bloodshed for both human and M'Nae, and must be avoided.

Ken sent his feeble mental appeals wider afield, to someone with more authority than Thayenta possessed. *Don't do it, Briv. Bide your time. Give us a chance to work this out. Please!*

"Sha . . . shalessa?" Thayenta said in a quavering, little-girl voice. It was persuasive, because Thayenta was really scared. Wanting to comfort her, he formed a picture—himself, R.C., and Thayenta shoulder to shoulder, united against the foe. As a guide, he added a mini-drama of Thayenta cowering in front of Eads, but guarded, wary and observing.

A *yes* winged back to him, telepathically. The sound of the word, echoed in Ken's skull. She had heard and understood him!

Now he had to make sure her trust wasn't misplaced. He and R.C. had to protect the little alien with their lives if necessary. "It's a mistake," he soothed, as much for the onlookers as Thayenta. "They won't hurt you anymore, honey."

"Chief, should we—"

"It's all right, Greer," Eads dismissed the club wielders. "You boys get back to your posts. Keep an eye out for any more of 'em—and bring 'em to me. I'll take care of this one."

As they drifted back up the trail Eads gazed intently at Thayenta. His taut, wide-eyed stare disturbed Ken. An odd little half-smile twisted Eads' mouth. The man was unpredictable. Not even R.C. would know what to expect of his former classmate, now.

What should Ken tell Thayenta, telepathically? Warn her to be ready for anything? How could he explain that they were dealing with a human who was unstable, an outlaw by human legal standards?

Abruptly, Eads took Thayenta's chin in his strong fingers and turned her head to catch the sunlight best. He examined her closely, and Thayenta bore his rudeness without comment, though Ken felt her tremble.

No, don't call Briv for help. Not . . . yet!

"Yes, yes! Definitely one of them," Eads concluded. "I thought maybe she might be a member of a third species. Some native I hadn't spotted during my Initial Survey. But she's one of the invaders. Same peculiar skin and black eyes . . ."

"She befriended us," R.C. said firmly, "and helped us after we were shipwrecked, lost in that mist. She led us to you and all she got for it was a beating from one of your men."

"The boys might have been too hasty," Eads said, smiling benignly. He had a lot of charm, almost enough to persuade Ken he had jumped to conclusions. But the glitter in those gray eyes was much too bright. "You must come down to the village, R.C. I insist you enjoy our hospitality, meager though it is. It gets damned hot here in the late afternoon, and the little lady must be uncomfortable. We'll find something for that bruise. If she can't walk—"

"I can help her," and Ken took Thayenta's arms, lifting her to her feet. She swayed slightly and leaned on him. R.C. offered a hand, but Ken waved the older man off.

"Youngsters," and R.C. smirked genially at Eads. "Think they can do anything."

Eads threw an arm across Zachary's shoulder, completely accepting this reunion with his old friend. Ken would have been happier to see more suspicion and a little honest distrust. Eads couldn't have been convinced. Not *that* easily.

The elite guards swung aside to let Eads and his "guests" pass, then closed in behind them. They followed Ken, R.C., and Thayenta down the trail.

Which one had killed the M'Nae ambassador, or had the killer been Eads himself?

The colonists had cannibalized some of the cargo ship's ruined plates. Diverting the natural channel of the falls, these formed blades for a crude water wheel. A bulky, old-fashioned storage chamber soaked up the slowly generated energy produced by the wheel.

Eads waved expansively, showing off his people's workmanship, and pointed to the earthen dam containing a small pond.

"Reservoir. We did it ourselves, R.C. It was a hell of a lot of work, but it'll be worth it in the drier season. It makes you feel proud to do it with your hands, too," Eads said, grinning broadly.

They reached the foot of the trail and walked across the valley floor. Ken kept his pace slow, pretending that Thayenta needed a little caution, although she was no longer trembling. Fascinated, he took in everything he could.

Groves of pink-leaved willows grew along the stream's banks, and the stream widened as it flowed through the valley. A scent of freshly-turned earth wafted on the breeze coming from the fields.

The men and women working the fields looked up and waved respectfully as Eads passed them. He was their revered leader. That was no hollow phrase, for all the people—the goons with the clubs, Eads' Praetorian guards, the colonists working the fields— looked upon Noland Eads as a demi-god. His word was law in this valley.

The field workers toiled over shallow furrows, breaking clods with hand rakes, pulling plows with human labor. Ken stared at the sight. Surely they couldn't have lost all their supplies and powered equipment in the crash. Could these people have chosen to revert to mankind's primitive farming methods?

"There's food and water at our community center," Eads said, gesturing toward the little village. Heading toward the stream, Ken, R.C., and the alien woman followed him onto a well-travelled lane between two of the fields. "Imagine you'd like to get in out of this sun for a while. You been travelling far, R.C.?"

"A while," R.C. replied evasively. "It's difficult to judge distance when all your instruments are gone." Zachary was a good liar when he had to be.

"Right, right!" Eads wasn't troubled by his classmate's evasion. Murmers rippled through the fieldworkers as they saw Thayenta. Eads waved reassuringly to them, calming their fears. Noland Eads had everything well in hand.

Ken read the colonists' expression. Thayenta was an alien, a telepath. An object of hatred. Noland Eads wasn't the only xenophobe here, merely the most prominent.

He counted heads. Three dozen colonists working the fields, perhaps two dozen more busy constructing buildings. There might be others on the far side of the village. And Eads had posted quite a few guards.

At this point, the NE 592 population balance favored the Terrans, not the M'Nae. But the M'Nae claimed to be here first. A few telepaths against dozens of armed and edgy humans. The outcome would be anyone's guess.

Eads clumped over a quaint wooden footbridge spanning the stream. Ever the genial host, he pointed out sights along the village's "main street." "We're just getting started, of course, but she'll be solid as a rock when we get through. We've used nothing but native wood and materials, R.C.," and he indicated the log and flagstone construction, the window-less buildings.

Ken and R.C. were intrigued by certain unique qualities of this pioneer village. "Did you lose your force tools in the crash?" R.C. asked.

"We didn't bring any!" Eads sneered, and he and his Praetorians shared a loud, private joke at the Surveymen's expense. Eads went on, "we don't need them. Technology is the curse of humanity: it saps us, sucks us dry, makes us soft and weak."

"You've been saying that for years, Noland," R.C. said lightly, unimpressed by the sermon.

"Yes, for years, and nobdy would listen to me. Nobody would act on it." Eads stomped to the village's central building and scuffed across a hand-planed door sill. The interior looked dark, and Ken and R.C. hung back, not eager to enter a cul-de-sac. Eads halted on the threshold and grinned wickedly at them. "What are you afraid of? Come on!"

What was that old proverb? *Walk into my parlor, said the spider to the fly.* A chill chased up the back of Ken's neck. But there was nothing they could do—not against men armed with needlers. R.C. followed Eads inside and Ken helped Thayenta through the door. The Praetorians brought up the rear.

THE building was a log and stone fortress and housed a single large room filled with wooden benches and tables. A great deal of labor had gone into its construction. Eads was right. With the shutters propped open it *was* cooler inside. Natural air conditioning carried through the odors of grass and plowed earth.

But since the shutters didn't admit much light, the interior was dark and shadowy. Ken assumed these colonists used candles at night, faithful to Eads' back to the primitive philosophy.

"Our community center," Eads explained, exhibiting the rough-hewn open beams supporting the roof. "We did it all ourselves."

Their escort remained. Protecting their leader against treachery, two Praetorians stood by the door and the other circled behind Eads. Obviously they didn't trust the Surveymen.

"Sit down, sit down!" Eads invited, waving to the benches. Ken showed Thayenta what to do. She was childishly delighted, and plainly she'd never seen Terran furniture before, which explained why the rock and plastic cell at M'Nae headquarters was so bare of the amenities.

Eads shoved a pitcher and cups, a bowl of bread-stuffs and fruit across a table toward his uneasy guests. "Here. Have a snack, a cup of cool stream water. There are few toxic flora on this planet, remember. I checked the place out myself, very thoroughly, a while back." He chuckled at his own humor then bit noisily into a piece of the fruit, playing king's taster to allay their suspicions.

Ken poured a cup of water for Thayenta, urging her to drink. The bruise on her cheek looked bad. If she had suffered any shock, she ought to take fluids. As the woman sipped, Ken pulled a rag off his torn sleeve and dipped a corner in another cupful of water, gently daubing at her cheek with the makeshift swab.

"How much *do* you remember, R.C.?" Eads suddenly asked. He leaned forward, eagerly awaiting Zachary's answer.

"Of what? Your theories on modern man's decadence?" R.C. parried. "I remember that well—so does everyone else who ever served with you. Sometimes it was hard to tell when the theories quit and Noland Eads began." R.C. pretended to relax, lolling on the bench. "Every time we touched down on an uninhabited world, you saw it as a potential new beginning—man on his own in combat with the elements."

"It's true!" Eads brought his fist down hard on the table, making the cups dance. His craggy features were contorted, his demeanor, demoniacal.

"No special weapons or tools," R.C. muttered, quoting from the past. "How do you explain those needlers? I don't consider *that* meeting nature on her own terms. Or do you expect nature to arrive at the head of an army, Noland? You intend to use those against wild game?"

Eads planted a boot on the bench beside R.C. and rested his elbows on his knee. When he grinned, the tension in the room took a quantum leap. "Maybe. Or maybe they're useful against something a lot more sophisticated than wild game."

"Such as the Patrol when they eventually find you? And they will," R.C. said levelly.

Eads' grin widened into a nasty leer. "I never did answer your first question, did I, R.C.? Funny. That was always *your* trick—stalling, never quite getting around to a straight answer." He broke into a cackle, slapping his thigh with a smack that made Thayenta start and nearly drop her cup. Taking it from her fingers, Ken replaced it on the table.

The leader of the marooned colonists began pacing back and forth. Eads' great head swivelled, and he never took his eyes off his old classmate. "Yes, I learned from you, R.C. Many, many things. You're a damned good pilot. The best. Just one of your specialties I was happy to borrow. But you never would learn from me, would you? You wouldn't listen when I told you how man was really *meant* to live out here on the frontier."

"I listened," R.C. said with apparent sincerity. He took Eads aback.

"Did you? I hope you did, R.C. That means there's a chance." Coming to a stop, he licked his lips and confronted Zachary. "Then tell me—how close *is* Earth Central to pinpointing my colony world?"

The atmosphere in the room grew heavy with menace, and Thayenta wriggled close to Ken. She sensed it telepathically. All the human conversation must be gibberish to her ears, but she could read the emotions.

So could Ken. Violence lurked right under the surface.

"I'm not sure what you're talking about," R.C. began, temporizing.

Without preamble Eads backhanded the Surveyman, sprawling Zachary forcefully back against the bench.

Fists clenched, Ken rose to lunge to R.C.'s aid, but strong fingers bit into his collarbone. Turning, he saw a needler aimed at his head. On the other side, the second guard pointed his weapon at Thayenta.

Ken froze, infuriated and helpless! His mind raced through possibilities, desperately seeking some plan to save them.

"Answer me!" Eads screamed at Zachary. "I know all your tricks, R.C. I'm not stupid, and I know the Patrol isn't. I need time. A year, two years, five. Then we'll own this planet. We'll have won it with our bare hands, the way it should be won. It'll be too late for Earth Central to uproot us then. I've got connections in high places, R.C. When my friends pull the right strings, they won't *dare* send the Patrol in here. NE 592 is ours. If they try to take it away from us they'll hear the explosion all the way back to Earth!"

He was actually raving, his face red, his eyes bulging. Ken was appalled. A living legend like Noland Eads—come to this. Too many dangerous and stressful missions out into nothingness had caused this breakdown.

That backhanded blow had split R.C.'s lip. Blood dabbled down to his chin. Zachary made no effort to wipe it away. He gazed pityingly at Eads, saying nothing.

Enraged by the silence, Eads grabbed Zachary's fatigues, shaking the Surveyman. "Tell me! How much time have we got? How much time!"

With amazing calm, R.C. grasped Eads' wrists. Their eyes met in a battle of wills. Then either R.C. broke Eads' steely grip, or Eads chose to let go. Ken exhaled slowly as R.C. palped his swollen lip. With scorn he mopped the blood off and said, "You're up against it now, Noland."

"What?" Eads raised his hand to strike again, but held it in check.

Ken felt like a coiled spring, his anger poised on a trigger. If Eads hit the captain again, could Ken stop himself from leaping at the man?

Unperturbed, Zachary sounded as if he were reading from a briefing tape. "They spotted all of it back at Earth Central, Noland. The missing Class-D cargo ship. The missing supplies, the stolen needlers. And your colonists. Oh, those were obvious, too. They stood out like sore thumbs on the missing-persons listings. All those kooks and fanatics and drop-outs who'd joined the Old-Ways Sect disappeared.

A spasm of pain shot through Ken's shoulder as the guard's grip tightened. R.C.'s crack about "kooks" had scored. It would take a shipful of fanatics to follow Noland Eads out to NE 592 in this mad, illegal scheme.

"Go on! Go on! What else?" Eads said. Some of the frenzy died out of him, replaced by burning curiosity.

"It didn't take long to put all the pieces together," R.C. went on with maddening placidity. "It was plain you had engineered the ship theft and manipulated the requisition sheets in order to supply this colony. The *type* of supplies gave you away from the start, Noland: hand tools. And you had far too many 'colonists' to control. Some of them couldn't resist bragging in letters to their friends and relatives— hinting about the great adventure coming up, their conversion to the Old-Ways Sect, and Noland Eads' philosophy."

"But Earth Central couldn't know where we were going!" Eads shouted in triumph. "They couldn't begin to know that. It's a big galaxy. We could have gone anywhere. They won't find us for years!"

"Why not?" R.C. said in that same dispassionate tone. "I did."

Eads boggled at him, and Ken cast a sidelong glance at his guard. Not yet. Their attention was divided, but not sufficiently. It was still too risky to break for it.

"How?" Eads sounded betrayed, a hurt, spoiled brat whose secret hiding place was obvious to an adult.

"You said you learned from me," R.C. said. "The reverse is true, whether you believe it or not. Knowing you, it wasn't difficult."

"A stab in the dark! It had to be!" Eads clung to his insistence that his plan was foolproof, undetectable. "It was an accident that you came to NE 592."

R.C. granted him the thinnest of smiles. "Figure it out for yourself, Noland." He let the suspense hang for several long seconds, and Eads' mania to know ripened. Finally R.C. said, "All right. You had to have chosen a primitive world. I ran a computer check for water balance, timber, the "proper proportion" of predators to prey—proper according to Noland Eads' philosophy, which I knew well. I listened to your speeches, and I don't forget things, Noland. You forget a lot of things. You don't consider all the possibilities, and sometimes that can be fatal."

The needlers aimed at Ken's and Thayenta's heads drooped slightly, and the grip on Ken's shoulder lessened still more. The guards were rapt, hypnotized by R.C.'s performance. The odds were getting better, but the moment had still not come. The man protecting Eads' back was enthralled, but he was three or four meters away, safe from easy attack.

"I don't . . ." For the first time doubt crossed Eads' homely face. He drew back, frowning at R.C. "Earth Central *can't* know. You're just whistling to keep your spirits up."

A chuckle rumbled in R.C.'s throat. "You're the one with problems, not me, Noland. You were beaten before you ever lifted ship for this planet."

"We both know the way Patrol operates," Eads flared. "They're not going to act on this immediately —even if you did pinpoint NE 592, which I don't believe. You gave them a couple of dozen options on my hideaway world. They never will be able to decide which one you picked to investigate first, or second, or—"

"I wasn't speaking of the Patrol," R.C. said somberly. "Earth Central doesn't figure into this, now. You're up against a random element, one not even Noland Eads predicted. And that element's going to finish your colony."

Eads set his acne-scarred jaw. "Nothing's going to stop us. What the hell are you babbling about?"

"The M'Nae." Zachary dropped the explanation

casually. As Eads and the guards puzzled over it, R.C. shot a get-ready glance in Ken's direction. Like an Academy lecturer bored with his material, R.C. went on, "The aliens. The M'Nae. That's what they call themselves."

"That woman," and Eads glowered hatefully at Thayenta.

"She's unimportant. Only one of many." R.C. shook his head pityingly. "You're worrying about small fry. It's too late for that. The M'Nae got to this planet before you did, Noland. You invaded their territory—their territory by prior right. Even by Earth's legal standards, their claim is valid, and it pre-dates yours. Their colony was here before you crashed. The M'Nae sent an ambassador to negotiate with you, and you killed him. They send you a second one, and your goons maul her."

Eads' mouth was open and the guards were nonplussed. R.C. rammed the point home. "Killing an ambassador is a very serious crime—particularly for a colony established by illegal means. An alien ambassador. In every culture we've known, the person of an ambassador is inviolate. Noland, you just may have triggered an interplanetary and interspecies war."

CHAPTER 9

Eads acted swiftly. He whirled, drawing his needler, thumbing back the intensity control, preparing to fire a deadly lance into Thayenta.

Ken's own reflexes were equally quick, however. He tackled the alien woman, knocking her to the floor. "Down! Keep down!" He prayed she'd understand. No time to worry about the hidden translator, or about sending telepathic images to her!

R.C. threw himself on Eads, wrestling his former friend for the illegal weapon.

At the same instant Ken swung his arms wide, locking his elbows, and the guards to either side were smashed across their throats. They doubled over, gagging in pain.

Ken charged past R.C. and Eads. The third guard was wavering, trying to aim his needler but afraid of hitting Eads by mistake. Ken drove a boot into the man's solar plexus and sent him sprawling.

The needler! It sailed off into the room's shadows. No chance of finding it without a search.

Ken landed a solid punch on the guard's chin,

knocking the man out for the moment. Then he spun on his heel.

R.C. was holding his own. The wiry Surveyman lacked Eads' height and strength, but desperation and sanity evened the struggle. One of the guards was coming to, fumbling for the needler he had dropped.

Ken leapt across overturned benches blocking his path. He had to stop that guard before. . . .

"The woman!" Eads gasped. "Shoot the woman!"

R.C. forced Eads' weapon hand down. The colony leader squeezed the trigger several times, and needler darts set the floorboards smoldering.

"She's their tool! Their eyes! You've got to kill her!" Eads ranted.

A guard was raising his weapon to level at Thayenta as Ken crashed into him. They went down in a pummeling heap. At the impact, the needler bounced out of the Praetorian's hand, but he was a capable rough-and-tumble fighter. He gave as good as he got. Fists and knees and head butts flew fast and furious.

Ken caught a glimpse of the two older men waltzing around in a macabre dance, locked in a life and death battle. "Kill her! Kill them all!"

"Listen to me!" R.C.'s voice was wrenched in gasps by effort. "Noland! Listen! There's too many of them! You've got to—"

Appeal for reason was useless. Eads' twisted mind burned with a lust for violence and death. Death for the alien woman and her kind, death for anyone who helped the M'Nae.

Ken dodged a punch and countered with a hard

one of his own, rattling the Praetorian's head off the floor. Semi-conscious, Eads' guard was a sitting duck for the finishing blow.

Ken snatched up the needler the man had dropped earlier. The remaining guard, still coughing, was struggling to draw a bead on Thayenta.

Thayenta had huddled beside a bench throughout the melee. She was wide-eyed, stunned by the physical behavior of the humans. Their motives were an enigma, alien. Ken—a friend—had knocked her down and she'd stayed put.

Ken jumped over a bench and threw a body block into the last guard. The two of them reeled back into the log and flagstone wall. The Praetorian took the brunt of the shock. Glaze-eyed, he slithered to the floor in a limp heap.

Ken grabbed the man's needler, thrust it in a pocket, and hurried toward Thayenta.

A sizzling noise ripped through the large room. An ugly sound, one Ken had previously heard only on tapes.

R.C. uttered a strangled cry, jerking away from Eads. Clutching his left leg, the Surveyman toppled, writhing from the agony of a needler hit.

Ken froze as Eads turned, weapon in hand.

Then, purposefully, Ken raised his confiscated needler and pointed it at Eads' leonine head. "Hold it right there."

Eads was aiming too—not at Ken, but at Thayenta.

The deadly tableau held them all immobile for five or six heartbeats.

R.C., muffling a groan, dragged himself along the floor, reaching a hand up to Eads. "Noland, don't! Listen to me!"

A charred patch on R.C.'s fatigues oozed blood. Pain twisted at Zachary, but he thrust it aside for a more critical matter. He pleaded for understanding. "There's too many of them, Noland. A whole planet of them, more coming through all the time. Killing the woman won't solve anything. It'll only make it worse!"

Truth, lies, and speculation mingled wildly in a frantic attempt to stay Eads' murderous drive.

Ken's finger rested lightly on the needler trigger. He could deal death, but if he did, so might Eads. The man's madness made it all a terrible gamble. Even with a needler ray through his brain, Eads might pull the trigger.

While R.C. begged his old friend to see reason, Ken cleared his mind. One small section focussed on Eads, on the needler in Eads' hand, but the remainder . . . Ken didn't dare look at Thayenta. He mustn't take his eyes from the madman confronting him. Yet he could *think* in Thayenta's direction.

Telepathy. It wasn't an interesting experiment this time. Their lives depended on Ken's ability to project his thoughts to the woman.

He had to create images. Thayenta could not grasp enough of his language to permit anything else.

Ken built mental pictures of Briv and the M'Nae council in the room with the prismatic alien matter transmitter. He concentrated on Briv, painting the M'Nae leader's image, hoping personal dislike did not cloud the telepathic impression. He portrayed Briv in the alien council chamber and simultaneously here, invisibly, in the illegal Terran colonist community center. Briv was a powerful telepath, able to teleport himself or objects, able to claw his way into a human mind.

If Briv *were* eavesdropping, observing, watching everything that had happened to his ambassador and the two Surveymen. . . .

Thayenta. Ken projected her image, in vivid and attractive detail. Then, though it hurt, he produced a cruel drama—Eads firing that needler. Thayenta, in pain, bleeding the same frothy pink blood Ken had seen covering the first ambassador's corpse. Then, most difficult of all, he imagined Thayenta dead.

Savagely, he wiped away the tragedy. It mustn't happen! But it would if Briv didn't help!

The M'Nae had to become allies. Ken and R.C. were fighting not only for their own lives but those of so many others, M'Nae and human.

Briv had to help! And quickly!

Ken's stare was riveted on Eads, on the needler and a tense trigger finger. In a moment, those guards would regain consciousness. A colonist might wander by the community center and peer inside to see what was happening. Then Eads would have more than enough reinforcements to finish his bloody work.

Ken winged another telepathic message toward Thayenta, and beyond her, to Briv. Just how strong *was* Briv? Could he not "hear" Ken's communication? Why didn't the M'Nae leader act?

R.C., somehow finding the strength, had levered

himself up to his good knee. He continued to hammer at Eads, gently, with words. Wounded and weaponless, words were all Zachary possessed.

Miraculously, Eads' expression slowly shifted. A peculiarly vacant gaze replaced the bug-eyed frenzy. Shakily, Eads lifted his free hand and rubbed his forehead. He looked dizzy, disoriented.

Suddenly, outside the building, a loud clanging started. An alarm bell? Ken tensed at the sound and barely kept himself from squeezing the needler trigger.

Eads appeared deaf to the noise. As if he had fallen into a daydream, his gaze was unseeing, unreacting.

Or a telepathic trance!

Briv was reaching out from the M'Nae fortress in the mist.

"R.C.?" Whispering, careful not to wake Eads from that blank stare, Ken said, "I think the M'Nae have come over to our side."

"I see." The pilot was breathing heavily, using the bench for support, gradually pulling himself up onto his right foot. Blood drenched his pant leg below the left knee. Gritting his teeth, he hobbled a few steps, moans escaping him as he jostled the wounded limb.

Still training his "borrowed" needler on Eads, Ken dug in his pocket for the M'Nae translator. He held out the metallic oblong to Thayenta. "Here. Quick. We've got to be able to communicate in a hurry!"

She got up and ran to him, seizing the translator. Her dress of living material instantly grew a necklace to support the device once more. Thayenta slipped it onto the glittering thong and said, "Briv has stopped the death-bringer . . . for a while. He will confuse their minds, for a while."

"Doesn't he realize what we're up against?" Ken said hoarsely. "It can't be for just 'a while'. It has to be permanently. The minute Briv lets go, Eads will return to the same madness. He's determined to kill all the M'Nae."

Troubled, her large eyes moist, Thayenta said, "For a while Briv is watching. You must . . . make the death-bringers leave."

"We can't! Their ship's wrecked, just like ours. Humans can't teleport from one planet to another."

"Ken," R.C. said heavily. "You're right, but we haven't the time."

"Okay!" Ken looked at Thayenta, trying to read a response to his explanation.

"Can . . . can not," she said, slumping. "For a while." She hesitated. Possibly the telepathic message she had received was too depressing to repeat. Finally Thayenta blurted, "We must help ourselves. Briv will watch, send mist to confuse the death-bringers—"

"But only for a while," Ken finished, repeating the key phrase in Briv's strategy. "Thayenta, have him teleport you out of here. You can get away. R.C. and I will manage on our own."

Tears brimmed on Thayenta's black eyelashes. She looked frightened. "I do not . . . know how. I am a . . . student."

"Dammit, Briv can teleport you out of here!" Ken gazed around angrily, addressing the air, the invisible presence of the M'Nae leader. "You can't be that cold-blooded. We aren't going to betray you. She doesn't need to watch us like a hawk and risk getting killed. Get her out of here. Please!"

There was no reply. Thayenta bit her lip, snuffling back tears. Briv was not going to remove Thayenta from the line of fire.

Briv certainly was no fool. He had seen Eads in motion. And if the alien could not see that the colonists' leader was insane, he still must understand that these were his enemies, potential attackers. Briv was using Thayenta as a spy, readying for that attack.

Did he intend to pit ten M'Nae against dozens of colonists armed with needlers?

"Noland," R.C. said mournfully, "what have you done? What the hell have you done? An interstellar war. You're totally out of your league. Your philosophy's no good. You're going to get yourself and all these colonists killed."

"He can't hear you," Ken said. Ordinarily R.C. would have seen that, but pain was muddling his mind. "No! Don't, R.C.!" The pilot had reached out to touch Eads' arm. At Ken's shout, Zachary aborted the gesture, recognizing the danger.

Ken studied Eads' blank face a few seconds more, then lowered his needler. So long as Briv held the man in that telepathic trance, the weapon was unnecessary.

One of the guards mumbled, waking up. Ken applied one last jab to the man's jaw. "We'd better get out of here," he suggested.

"Yes!" Thayenta agreed, urgently tugging at Ken's remaining sleeve. "Now!"

Ken hurried to R.C., slung the captain's arm over

his shoulder. "Come on. You can't reach Eads. Give it up."

"All right." He leaned heavily on Ken as they lurched toward the door. Ken paused on the threshold, assessing the situation outside.

CLOUDS of purplish mist wafted through the little village and across the plowed fields.

If they used it well, it could serve as a smoke screen for Thayenta and the Surveymen. There were some colonists a short way down the village main street. They were waving their arms with great agitation, arguing about the strange mist.

Grateful for the delay, Ken asked, "Thayenta, how much time before Briv takes back his purple fog?"

"Two . . . two valia," she said, then made a small noise Ken interpreted as self-disgust, annoyed with herself for her inability to convert M'Nae to human terms.

"Long time?" Ken pleaded. "Or short?"

She held her hands half a meter apart, and struggled to find a word. "In . . . middle," Thayenta said, looking apologetic. She pointed northeast, toward the water wheel and the trail leading to the stream. "We go back to M'Nae."

"We'd never make it," R.C. warned. He sagged, and Ken took a firmer purchase on the man's arm.

Forced to agree, Ken said, "No, not likely. We'll never get through unless Briv has incapacitated every single guard along the way, Thayenta."

She caught his meaning and imitated a human's negative head shake. "No. They are confused. Only

Wild-Eyes, the chief death-bringer, is held without thought."

"Eads," Ken guessed. "Briv's put him in some kind of trance—for a while. We're on our own as far as the rest of the colonists go."

R.C. was silent, breathing hard, and functioning on courage alone. Most of his weight was now carried by Ken. Suddenly Ken exclaimed, "The ship! Guards will be watching for us to make a break toward the trail—not in the other direction. There must be plenty of hiding places in a Class-D cargo carrier. Can you make it that far, Captain?"

Sweat dotted R.C.'s brow. Somewhere he found the strength to say, "If I can't, leave me. You and the girl get away. I'll take my chances arguing Noland into a truce—"

"Maybe." Ken wouldn't put any bets on that. But there was no time to debate the matter. "Thayenta, see that lane going between these two buildings? You go down there and keep out of sight. Hurry."

She answered him with a sweetly encouraging smile. The bruise on her cheek only added to her piquant beauty, making her look more vulnerable. She ran to the alley between the community center and an adjoining stone and log structure. In the drifting fog, she seemed to melt into nothing. Camouflaged by Briv's smoke screen, Thayenta clung close to walls, as inconspicuous as a wraith.

As the two men struggled to the narrow dirt lane, R.C. breathed through his teeth. Ken half dragged the pilot into the shadowy alley Thayenta had taken. The woman had reached the rear of the building and was on the lookout for guards or wandering colonists.

Briv's mist floated eerily, folding and unfolding itself like a living thing. For all Ken knew, it was. There was so much Ken and Thayenta could exchange, discovering each other's culture and peoples. They were disparate species, but held much in common.

If only Briv would teleport the three of them safely out of the colonists' village back to the room with the prism. Ken laughed bitterly at his own wish. When he was imprisoned in the M'Nae stronghold, he had longed for freedom. Now he wanted to return to that foggy haven.

"How's it going?" he asked R.C. gently. The pilot muttered that he was doing fine. He wasn't, but they were both trying to keep up their courage. "Hang on. It's not too far."

That was not precisely a lie. But every step of the way would seem a kilometer to the injured man. Ken hesitated, wanting to give R.C. as much rest as he could. Plainly Zachary was steeling himself for the ordeal ahead.

Briv had to sense, telepathically, that R.C. was in agony, but that cold-blooded bastard was indifferent. He studied and watched them like bugs impaled on pins. It was an excellent way for Briv to learn about humans without becoming too involved, but it was tough on his guinea pigs!

"Thayenta, the big ship, over that way," Ken instructed. "And remember to hide in the mist as we go along. Okay?"

Thayenta nodded and skipped into the mist, heading in the general direction of the wrecked Class-D. In her wake, Ken and R.C. moved awkwardly. A three-legged race bereft of all humor, theirs was a grim struggle to survive. R.C. wheezed heavily from his heroic efforts, and several times he almost slipped out of Ken's grasp, half-fainting. But each time he rallied, bravely hopping along, his bloody leg dragging.

On the grassy slope, the going became tougher. Ken waded through it on a zigzag course, seeking bare ground and keeping Thayenta in sight in the purple mist.

A pile of crumpled metal blocked Ken's path, and he laboriously detoured around it. Then there was another pile, and another from debris strewn in the wake of the Class-D's death slide into the valley. The colonists were collecting the junk, sorting it into piles to be salvaged later. They had already built the water-wheel from such scrap. They were fanatics, but also hardworking and resourceful. If only the colonists and the M'Nae could bury their differences.

"Must . . . be getting close," R.C. panted.

"Soon," Ken replied. In this fog, he couldn't gauge the distance accurately. The ground was rising slowly, gradually angling up toward the valley's back wall.

Yes, there it was! Ahead now, through a gap in the purple mist, Ken saw the immense bulk of the wrecked cargo ship.

More debris and storage dumps blocked their way —little pyramids of metal and plastic, much of it charred and fused into fantastic shapes by the terrible stresses of the crash.

Had the cargo ship suffered the same mysterious fire that destroyed the survey ship? How badly was she wrecked inside? Where would be the best place to hide themselves and avoid pursuit?

Ken searched his memories for a design diagram of a Class-D. He wished he had paid closer attention during those ship identification lectures back at the Academy. It was a hell of a time to need a refresher course! Then it hadn't seemed important, but it was essential now. Where were the hatches, corridors, all the nooks and crannies that could hide a wounded pilot, his apprentice, and an alien woman?

Although there was some distance yet to go before they'd reach her, the ship loomed above them. The forekeel was buried meters deep in the valley wall, which meant there was no chance to use the forward hatches. She was enmeshed in earth and grass and rocks up to the third-level. That would leave port and starboard and rear accesses.

R.C. grunted and gasped with each step as Ken helped the pilot along, taking it as slowly as he dared. Pursuers? He hadn't heard any . . . yet. The mist seemed to muffle sound as well as cloud vision.

Hunting a likely entryway, Ken studied the gigantic bulk of the Class-D. It could not be too far up the side. R.C. was unable to climb with his leg wound. And it could not be too obvious—nothing that would attract the attention of Eads and his people.

Thayenta scampered back to the two men, and the

purple mist swirled about the three of them. He heard faint shouts from their left. The words were garbled and unintelligible, but the tone was angry and excited.

Maybe somebody had discovered the direction of their escape.

Thayenta pawed through her meager Terran vocabulary a moment, then gave up and made use of her translator. "Where do we go, Ken?"

Ken glanced at R.C. The captain's gaze was dim-eyed and unfocussed, his lips lax as breath whistled past a dry throat. What was keeping the man conscious?

The ship was over a kilometer in length. The nearest access to Ken was an undamaged rear cargo door which would swing open onto the ship's glide tracks. The colonists must have used it to unload the cargo and people who had survived the crash.

He vetoed that. The entry was too wide, too open, too easy to spot.

The distant chase veered westward for a few chilling seconds. As Ken stood silently, listening to the shouts, he wished the three of them were invisible, not merely shrouded in purple mist.

"Starrett, you see 'em head for the trail?"

"Had to be that way."

"Aw, he couldn't see 'em if they fell on him!"

"Try the bridge!"

These were the shouts of men bent on vengeance, of colonists fanatically loyal to Noland Eads. It was a lynch mob.

"Jude, check the south fence. . . ."

The cries faded, drifting off in several directions, away from Ken and R.C. and Thayenta. They had at least a temporary reprieve.

"That was close," Ken whispered. "Come on."

He had to make up his mind quickly. R.C. was too weak to stand a lengthy trek around to the ship's starboard side. Ken settled on a small hatch, low on the port hull section, that was partially opened but battered into a lump. Between the hull and the remainder of the seal fitttings a narrow gap was visible. Above the hatch a mangled sheet of plating drooped over the broken lock forming a metallic curtain that nearly concealed the little entryway. In stark sunlight or evening shadows—such as now—the sheeting hid the door from all but the closest scrutiny. Ken could see it at only one angle and hoped that held true for any pursuers as well.

R.C. groaned softly, nearly unconscious. "Hang on," Ken repeated, fighting down his rage at Eads.

The metal around the small hatch was razor sharp, reshaped into jagged teeth by the crash. Ken signalled Thayenta to enter first. She slid past the pointed metal, easily bending her slender form away from sharp projections.

Ken risked some noise, kicking at the bent door. It was built to take the stresses of deep space travel, but sliding across the planet had ruptured the ship's integrity. The hatch gave a few centimeters.

Wary of those cutting edges, Ken edged gingerly into the opening, dragging R.C. along with him.

Metal plucked at Ken's fatigues and snagged the fabric on R.C.'s chest, but both men escaped laceration. Another second, and they were both inside.

The hatch led to a tiny storage compartment inside a lifeboat auxiliary area. Thayenta was standing in the center of the little room, staring around curiously. Her head was cocked, alert. Was she guarding against pursuers, or listening to telepathic orders from Briv?

Ken knelt and slid R.C.'s arm off his shoulder. He stretched the pilot full length on a table. The wound was as bad as Ken had feared; the needler had bored through R.C.'s calf muscles, and blood drenched his pant leg and covered the boot.

Ken ripped the cloth back from the wound as gently and carefully as possible. Even so, R.C. moaned. Ken started to tear a rag off his ruined sleeve to use as a tourniquet. But Thayenta stopped him.

Smiling at the injured pilot, she plucked her fingers at the hem of her pink garment. There was no ripping sound, no indication of damage to her clothes, but she suddenly had a neat roll of fluffy fabric in her hands. Thayenta bent over R.C.'s leg, using part of the material to wipe blood gently away from the wound.

"You've got some tricks no nurse ever had," Ken said admiringly. He winged a ten-second first aid course to her, telepathically. Thayenta offered him a strong strip of the pink material.

As a test, he snapped it, fascinated. Like Thayenta's clothing, the material left . . . alive. And yet it was fabric, as soft and pliable as an old-fashioned piece of gauze.

"Not. . . ." Thayenta imitated the act of spraying bandage. She remembered the medi-kit! And Ken recalled that sensation of someone invisible sitting beside him, pawing through the medi-kit's contents with him.

"No, it's not modern medical issue, but it will do," he smiled. Ken stripped off R.C.'s belt, made the man as comfortable as possible, then set to the painful work of applying a tourniquet.

As he tightened the pink fabric Thayenta had supplied, R.C. grabbed Ken's wrist. Despite his loss of blood, the pilot's grip was strong. Putting Zachary in a supine position had lessened shock but heightened his awareness and pain. His eyes were very bright, and sweat ran down his face. "Never mind about the leg, Ken. You've got to—"

"In a minute," Ken said. "We have to slow down the bleeding." Thayenta pillowed R.C.'s head on her lap, stroking his brow, her fingertips playing gently at his temples. Waves of concern and sympathy washed over Ken, and some of the tightness melted out of R.C. The woman must be blunting his pain, telepathically.

Ken finished the tourniquet and examined the results. To his relief the flow of blood abated. He used the pink fluff to cover the wound itself. There was no way to tell if the bone was broken.

Thayenta shook her head, again using a Terran gesture. "Not . . . bone. O—kay."

He grinned back at her. "You have X-ray telepathy too? The Terran medical people would love to hire you!" His own comment startled him. Yes, that was true. M'Nae medical abilities could heal human patients.

R.C. had not let go of Ken's wrist throughout the first aid, hampering his work. Now the pilot's fingers tightened, demanding Ken's attention. "You've got to get up top."

Ken said, "Communications? You think—"

"Noland . . . good spaceman. The best," Zachary said weakly. "He'd have carried full gear, even for this crazy scheme, just in case he needed a Mayday."

That made sense. "Got it, Captain. Sit tight."

"Watch for guards," R.C. whispered.

Ken pried the pilot's hand off his wrist gently, then showed him the two confiscated needlers. "Equalizers, Captain. Here," and he pressed one close to Zachary's right hand. "I can handle it. After all, I've had the top pilot in Survey to learn from."

"Not the top," R.C. sighed, letting Thayenta soothe him. "That's Noland."

"I don't think so," Ken said, meaning it. "He had a Class-D coming into NE 592. A lot more power, a lot of cushion. He didn't have to crashland a small two-man Survey ship safely."

R.C. didn't hear him, lulled into semi-consciousness. Ken propped a mashed storage locker under the pilot's feet, elevating his lower limbs to counter shock. He wished he had some sort of blanket to keep Zachary warm.

Immediately, Thayenta plucked at her clothes, stripping away more of the pink-leaved fabric. The remainder flowed out tenuously to cover her body. She was reduced to a wisp of nothing, and the results were distracting. Ken took her offering and tucked it around the injured pilot carefully.

"You're handy to have around," and he leaned across Zachary's limp form and kissed her lightly. Thayenta seemed puzzled, but intrigued by the gesture. "Stay with R.C. I'm going up higher in the ship to try to contact my people. My home world. Do you understand? Does Briv understand?"

She debated the matter, listening to orders from M'Nae headquarters, then nodded. Ken went on, "If you hear anyone, hide. Get out of here. Probably, they won't kill R.C.," he added lamely. Trying to make the argument solid, he added, "After all, we're human. But you're in danger, Thayenta."

Ken stared into empty air, addressing Briv directly. "If I can contact my home planet, my people will come and capture Eads. They will take him and the other death-bringers away and leave this world to the M'Nae. Please don't kill any of the colonists. Give me a chance."

There was no response. Thayenta was expressionless. If Briv was in agreement, he wasn't sharing it with his little ambassador.

Ken patted Thayenta's shoulder, then ran out of the compartment. Briv had to keep that smoke screen a while longer to protect R.C. and Thayenta.

He chased along corridors and clambered up glide

tubes that no longer operated. All the mechanical and electronic gear was either non-functioning or gutted. Eads' people had cannibalized what they could and left the rest for junk. But that shouldn't apply to communications. Possibly Eads wouldn't *want* to call for help, ever; but surely he would have kept radio equipment operating and repaired any damage. No one would deep-space without some insurance against unforeseen catastrophe.

Ken reached the ship's top deck and ran the full length. At the control section, he slowed his pace. There were no guards. Staring in numb horror, Ken stood in the door to Communications. There had been no cannibalizing of equipment, here: there was nothing to cannibalize.

R.C. was wrong. Eads had broken completely with all the rules, even those that kept a man alive in deep space. The communications room was absolutely clean. Along the bulkheads, where consoles should have stood, there was nothing but a few faint outlines to show where apparatus *had* been. The stark cleanliness of the spots, the sealed circuitry fixtures all pointed to one conclusion. The ship never carried deep space com gear!

This colony couldn't call for help. No matter how bad things got, the colony was voiceless.

There had been radar, a deep-space navigation tool, but after the crash, the colonists had ripped out its parts. But there was no way Ken could convert such equipment to warp frequencies anyway.

Eads' madness sliced at Ken like a knife. All of

them were on their own, permanently severed from the communications umbilical connecting them with home.

No reinforcements need be expected, now, or for months—years—to come.

CHAPTER 10

"I don't believe it." R.C.'s expression underlined his statement. "Nothing?"

"It was stripped clean. They must have done that as soon as they stole the ship from the Proxima berth," Ken said, reluctant to break the news and shatter R.C.'s hopes. As the pilot sat up, grim-faced, Ken grabbed his shoulders.

He tried to soften the news with a smile, but that wasn't necessary. Obviously R.C. was well aware of their position. "No, no, I'm fine," he reassured Ken. "I really do feel much better—thanks to the girl. The pain is down to an occasional twinge, and she even did something to take the swelling in my lip away."

Thayenta knelt by Zachary's side, looking pleased with herself. Ken acknowledged her skill with a nod and replied, "But a needler wound is still a serious injury."

The pilot tentatively wiggled his left foot. "It still hurts, but I'm sure I can walk. We got rid of the tourniquet and there's no further bleeding. I tell you,

Ken, if we can get the M'Nae together with some Terran doctors . . ."

"Right." Ken rummaged in a pocket and dug out a vial of old-style concentrates, dropping them into R.C.'s hand. "And here's some icing for the cake. I found them up top. The colonists hadn't cleaned out all the lockers."

Zachary flipped open the vial and hungrily popped several of the tablets. He made a sour face. "Old. They taste like they've been on board since this tub was commissioned."

"Probably have, but the nutritional value should be intact." Ken went to the hatchway and peered out, checking for search parties. The view downhill toward the village was clear of purple mist now and sundown shadows raked across the valley. There was no one in sight.

Zachary munched a few more tablets before offering some to Thayenta. She shook her head, amused. R.C. shrugged and said, "Yes, everything has to be 'natural' for Noland. Fits his philosophy. Naturally, he'd ignore these concentrates when his people stripped this ship. No communications, no force tools. He lectured on the natural life all those years, but none of us really thought he'd carry through on those harebrained ideas."

The little compartment was almost dark; only a small ray of light filtered in from rents in the bulkheads of adjoining compartments. R.C. propped himself up and tested his wounded leg again, thumping it lightly against the deck.

Thayenta said nothing. She must have been following some of the conversation, but what? Her lithe form was an elfin shadow in the fading light. How much of what Thayenta saw and heard was Briv learning as well? And what decisions would the alien leader make as a result?

"Did you tell Eads the truth?" Ken asked. "*Is* the Patrol likely to come hunting for him soon?"

"No, we can't expect much out of Central." It was too dark to see his face now, but Ken heard the regret in R.C.'s voice. "Once they were sure Eads had escaped, not rebelled, the assignment became a low priority. I had my own options on a search pattern. I was to locate him, if possible, and report back."

"So they could cart him back to Earth and turn him over to the psych people, I suppose. Would they lock him up and pry at his brains?"

"He's dangerous, Ken."

"Yes, but if he could be salvaged—"

"A brilliant mind is worse when it vectors off-center than a mediocre head is," R.C. quoted from a famous medical journal. He sighed, again worked his leg against the deck.

It was an eerie setting. They were in almost complete darkness, discussing the future of man and a complicated humanoid species, on the threshold of war.

Ken stared into the blackness. "Thayenta, why *did* our ship burn, and Ead's ship survive? He was the death bringer, not us."

She cocked her head to one side. In the faint light from the corridor Ken saw reflected iridescence out of the dark, two rainbow-colored circles: Thayenta's eyes, glowing. "I . . . we did not know he was the death bringer. Not at first."

Ken was entranced by her catlike gaze, but he forced himself back on course. "I see. And by the time we landed, you had decided that *all* humans were death bringers. So thanks to what Eads had done to your ambassador, we were attacked."

"It can't go any further," R.C. growled. "We've got to stop this insane collision."

Bitterly, Ken asked, "How? We have two needlers and a couple of days' supply of concentrates. That's our arsenal and food supply. Eads has a colony full of supplies. As for Briv. . . ." He paused, thinking over the meager information they had collected on the M'Nae. "Briv has his telepathy, and something called a Gera-ana. . . ."

Thayenta sucked in her breath, her cat's eyes glittering.

He had to get through to her. She was the key, the only link the Surveymen had. "You saved us, Thayenta. Briv could have wiped us out, but you saved us. You tried to warn me away, out in space. Then you pleaded our case when we crashed. Help us now. We've got to make Briv understand. There *can't* be war between M'Nae and humans. Even if the M'Nae win, a lot of them may die."

"Gera-ana," Thayenta repeated, slowly.

Ken fed M'Nae pronouncements back at her. "You said: we came here with the Gera-ana. I don't know if that means the big prism or the black area beyond the stream or the purple mist. But it's plainly something very important to the M'Nae. You know."

Ken had made several blind stabs, but Thayenta reacted as if he had laid bare the M'Nae's most closely guarded secrets. She gulped and said, "Briv—Vrytan. Very powerful. A walker between . . . places. He can be hard. Can break through shields if he desires."

"He'd have to be strong," R.C. mused. "It makes sense. The M'Nae came here from another world, and Briv's their leader. He'd have to be able to cope with anything that might crop up—even an encounter with an alien species."

"The pioneer breed." Ken smiled. It didn't make any difference that R.C. couldn't see him. "Just like a couple of men named Zachary and Eads. You know, if I think of Briv in *that* light, I just might be able to understand him and reason with him."

"Are you thinking of taking command?" R.C. asked. And after a short silence, he said firmly, "Agreed. You'll have to, Ken. This leg is better, but not good enough for any hard travelling. If anyone gets back to the M'Nae and settles this thing, it'll have to be you."

Ken argued, "If they come to the ship—"

"I can handle it." That sounded like the gruff and familiar R.C. Zachary, undaunted by a leg wound and a space wreck. "I've got a needler. And I cut my spaceman's teeth on Class-D cargo ships. I know this hulk inside out."

"She's dead," Ken warned. "No power, no elevators operational."

"I'm more at home in her than anyone out in that village, except Noland, and he's not in his right mind." R.C. hesitated, then said, "Go on, Ken. It's our best chance. I've got a stomach full of concentrates, and thanks to the lady, my leg feels better than it ought to. You go to the mountain, since it won't come to us."

R.C. was right. Ken was forced to agree that the choice was logical. "Are you sure?" he asked, loathe to leave the injured pilot.

"Go on," and R.C. slapped out at Ken, lightly striking the younger man's arm. "You've got a war to stop."

Ken stood up and heard—no, felt—Thayenta get to her feet. "I go, too," she said. "You must have guide to . . . to M'Nae. To the Gera-ana." She was reading Ken's mind, again, understanding his needs before he asked. He didn't resent her telepathic gifts so much any more. In fact, Ken began to revel in them. She was his ace in the hole, one Noland Eads couldn't hope to match.

"I would appreciate your help—one more time." Small fingers slid into his hand, warm flesh pressing his palm, a sweet fragrance filling the little compartment. This was the alien's response, not a scent of fear, but of trust.

"Good luck." In the dark, Ken and R.C. shook hands briefly. Both men knew the risks and accepted their share of them.

Towing Thayenta, Ken fumbled his way out into the dark corridor. The woman stumbled and gasped with annoyance, then steered him away from colliding with a bulkhead projection. "Not quite the blind leading the blind," Ken chuckled.

"Which way are we going?" Thayenta inquired via the translator.

Ken debated, then said, "Up high in the ship, toward the side where the sun sets. You can see in the dark, and I know the general construction of this ship; between the two of us we'll manage."

He was right. They teamed up with remarkable ease. Thayenta wasn't knowledgeable about compartment order or the location of ascent tubes, but she saw perfectly in the stygian guts of the cargo craft. Their progress was swifter than Ken had dared to hope. Occasionally he murmured, "There should be a corridor to the right about here," and felt a confirming tug on his hand by Thayenta.

FINALLY, they emerged on a level-two deck. Sifting through gaps in the hull, the last rays of daylight glimmered. Ken dug into his memories of Class-D specs. "Steering computers section. This'll do. There must be an access for antenna maintenance here."

The inner hatch was sprung from the crash. Now that his eyes served him once more, Ken pulled Thayenta along, hurrying across a suit locker. The suits were gone. The colonists must have taken them for the fabric. But the helmets still hung from their hooks. Several had been smashed in the wreck. They dangled facelessly, like skulls from the Terran technology that Eads and his people wanted to abandon.

Hydraulics were dead, so Ken had to crank the outer hatch manually: there was no sucking sigh as the last milliliters of oxygen rushed out into vacuum. But the air outside was fresher than the stale atmosphere in the dead ship.

Ken peered from the hatch warily, but there was

no sign of search parties. He had guessed well, choosing the starboard side and this level. A couple of meters below him the bulge of the ship's hull rested snugly against bare earth. The last rays of the setting sun sparked a golden radiance across the crest of the hill five meters above Ken's vantage point.

"Wait," he said, before stepping off the airlock's lip. He landed on all fours in the soft earth. Conveniently, the crash had jammed and loosened the soil, rendering it as pliable as sponge. He held up his arms and silently ordered Thayenta to jump. Without hesitation, she did.

Ken caught her easily, and held her a few moments longer than necessary. Sometime, there would be time to take things slowly. There were so many things he wanted to know about her.

In the twilight her features were ethereal, more lovely than ever, the bruise on her cheek almost unnoticeable. Her nose and brow wrinkled charmingly as she puzzled over his behavior.

They crept along the slope, heading for the valley's back wall. For part of the way they went on hands and knees. Dew was forming on the purple grass, making footing tricky and slippery.

Ken was alert, watching for guards. It was impossible to predict where Noland Eads might have posted them, but perhaps it hadn't seemed necessary to watch the village's back door. Eads figured the massive wreck of the ship was protection enough against invasion from that direction.

The reverse was true. From this angle the ship's bulk shielded them from any lookouts in the village.

And the valley's back wall was empty, unguarded. Ken helped Thayenta up the last meter or so of slope and they ducked under the shelter of a forest of pink willows.

The dying sun hung on the horizon for a last few seconds. Thayenta reached up to some low branches. To Ken's wide-eyed astonishment, the leaves flowed from the dangling limbs, became fabric. They twined and blended with the woman's wisp of clothing, replenishing the "cloth" she had donated as blankets and bandage for R.C.

"That's quite a little dress factory you've got there," Ken said admiringly.

Twilight descended, wrapping them in gray and violet. Light from NE 592's three moons dappled through the willow leaves, drenching the scene with multi-shadowed coolness, a beautiful, unreal world. Thayenta seemed to fit into it very well.

"I . . . I was cold," Thayenta said, apparently digesting Ken's comment.

"Whatever keeps you comfortable. We've got a long way to go tonight," Ken assured her softly. "I'm counting on you to steer that raft back upstream. Can you?"

A pause while her translator converted Terran words to M'Nae. But when Thayenta replied she scorned the device, speaking directly to Ken, copying his word. "I can."

"Good girl. Let's go." They started eastward, meandering through the lunar light, in and out of friendly, concealing willow trees. Ken felt oddly at one with nature, protected by the planet itself.

He almost persuaded himself he was on a lovers' stroll through a fantasy land. The grass was slightly damp, the air heavy and moist and perfumed with night flowers. Nocturnal insects and animals wakened and began a chirping chorus all about the two fugitives. It was hard to concentrate, in such a pleasant environment, hard to remember what must be done, the dangers he faced.

If he were out orbiting NE 592 in a Survey ship, it would all be cut and dried. There'd be no night sounds or scents, none of this intoxicating beauty. He would think in purely scientific terms: the terminator, the surface features, the spectroanalysis. Tape it and file it for reference.

But here, Ken was intensely alive, more aware of his senses than he had ever been before. Even facing possible death could not mask his heightened awareness of the alien loveliness around him and the nearness of Thayenta.

"If you get tired—" he started to say.

"I go. Thayenta go okay." She didn't use the translator, so he got the full effect of her irritation.

"Thayenta does indeed go okay," Ken agreed.

If she was wearied by all this heavy physical activity, she did not admit it. Her hand was firm on his, guiding Ken around fallen trees and marshy ground, under low hanging limbs. Now and then he caught a glimpse of moving lights to the left, down in the valley: search parties, still rummaging about.

Ken telepathically relayed instructions and Thayenta steered a wide course clear of the falls and the waterwheel. They cut across the circle. Ken drew maps in his head and let the alien woman pick his brain, enjoying the silent exchange, beginning to delight in the easy flow of information. He wordlessly explained his reasoning. *Best to come out of the woods well above the rapids, right at the place where they had beached the raft. That way they could avoid—*

There was a guard.

Ken pulled Thayenta down beside him in the lush grass and detritus of leaves dropped by willows. Fortunately they hadn't yet emerged from the woods. He pointed, winging his thoughts to that figure a few centimeters from his own. Her response came back. *Yes. I understand.*

Staying under the concealing droop of willow limbs along the bank of the stream, they crept upstream. Ken looked back to check their position. There was just one guard there, on the opposite bank, right where the raft was.

Frustrating! He hadn't counted on Eads reaching out that far to trap the fugitives. Okay. It would mean only a slight delay, if it was handled correctly.

They had come far enough. Ken gingerly stepped into the water, making as little splash as he could. The night was muggy, and the stream was comfortably cool. Thayenta was right behind him, unmindful of her clothes. Well, if she could make fresh dresses out of willow leaves any time she chose, he supposed she needn't trouble about a little dampness spoiling an outfit.

The current was sluggish here, well above the rapids. Ken waded slowly, glancing back at Thayenta frequently. The water was up to her waist, but she was earnestly following him to the opposite bank.

Ken telepathically ordered her to wait, then started back along the bank. Careful to make no noise, he let the night creatures mask his approach with their cheepings and rustlings in the willows.

The guard was using a torch pole staked down into the stream bank. He wasn't lucky enough to have an alien woman with cat vision to warn him of dangers.

Plainly the man had been on duty a long time. He was growing bored, inattentive, and eager to change watches and get back to the village. He probably assumed all the excitement was taking place in the valley and longed to join the search for Eads' enemies. The guard idly smacked a club into a cupped palm.

Ken slipped out from beneath the willows and stood an arm's-length from the guard. The man's back was to him.

Balancing lightly on the balls of his feet, Ken tapped the man's right shoulder.

"What the——?"

As anticipated, the man swung, backhanding the club in a wild arc. Ken ducked and drove a one-two punch into the man's middle. It took away both the man's fight and the breath he might have used to yell for reinforcements. Ken chopped down on the man's wrist, jolting the club loose. Then he brought his locked fists down on the guard's shoulder blades, collapsing the man into the grass.

There was no further movement. The man breathed deeply, evenly, but he was unconscious.

Well-satisfied, Ken tossed the club into the bushes nearby. One guard down, and no need for bloodshed. The man would come to with a sore stomach and an aching neck but no serious damage was done.

Ken had been tempted, though. He had recognized the face—one of the men who'd jumped his trio that afternoon. But he was *not* the man who'd struck Thayenta.

Thayenta was crying, like an abandoned kitten.

He tensed, looked downstream, on the alert. No one had heard his struggle with the guard. No one seemed to hear Thayenta. Ken hurried to her side, concerned.

She was crouched at the stream's bank, holding something . . . a piece of white . . . raft. There were a lot of other pieces of the same stuff, scattered along the reeds and under the willows.

No single piece was larger than Ken's hand. The thing had been battered to pieces. Eads' men, venting their spleen, had smashed the raft, reducing it to tiny fragments.

How would he and Thayenta get back to M'Nae headquarters now? Without the raft, it would take hours to trek upstream.

Then Thayenta's weeping hit him. These were not a human woman's tears. Deeper, they wrenched at Ken as if he himself were suffering some terrible, unbearable grief.

She rocked back and forth, cuddling the broken pieces of the raft. Whimpering. "Juissa. Juissa. Lao . . . lao . . ."

Her anguish ripped at Ken. He felt the pain of

loss, as real as if he shared the horror Thayenta would have felt had she found one of her people lying dead beside the river.

Ken's thought hit him like a physical blow. *Dead.* The raft was dead, and Thayenta was mourning it! How often he had puzzled over those M'Nae garments, wall surfaces and rafts, saying to himself, "The damned stuff acts like it's alive!"

It was!

Thayenta made her garments out of living things. All the M'Nae formed garments of natural objects, forming and reforming them, but never cutting or destroying.

They used willows or moss or something that became white plastic and undulated and breathed like living tissue.

In the harsh, wavering light of the torch, Thayenta's tears were diamonds, sparkling on the long lashes framing those space-black eyes. She looked up at Ken, and there was mingled rage and horror in her piquant face. By now she had learned quite a bit of Ken's language. The words that came at him were Terran, undiluted by the impersonality of the translator. "Kill! Death bringers. They kill! *Again!*"

CHAPTER 11

This was far more than a woman's grief over a slaughtered pet. Ken pulled Thayenta close, soothing her, empathizing with her torment.

She hammered small fists against his chest. Brokenly, she sobbed over and over, "Death bringers, death bringers. . . ."

The awful paradox twisted at Ken. There was Eads, whose philosophy demanded that man work hand in hand with nature, scorning technology, demanding a return to mankind's primitive days. On the other hand, the M'Nae—Eads' enemies, by the sheerest of accidents—were living hand in hand with nature, without any apparent technology, using the very stuff of the planet for their clothing and transportation.

"Thayenta, easy," Ken whispered. Even in this emotional turmoil, her cries were soft, unlikely to carry far in this damp air. There was no danger that the guards downstream might hear her. Ken let her cry it out, angry that she should have such pain, wishing he could explain human motives. The men who had "killed" the raft hadn't meant to be cruel, hadn't realized it was a living object.

171

Gradually, her weeping died, and Thayenta pushed away from Ken, staring at him with a bright, angry gaze. Fragile, and alien, she had never appeared so unhuman. The fury in her face startled him. "Kill. They always kill."

He had to bring the truth to her. "But the M'Nae have killed too, Thayenta. They've killed Terrans."

She gasped, her eyes widening. "M'Nae do not—"

"Yes, they do, not intentionally, but they do. Some of Eads' colonists died when the ship crashed and the ship crashed because of the M'Nae," Ken explained as simply as possible. "The Gera-ana, the shadow of the Iontran . . . whatever you call that place with the prism kills men. From space it's a blurry area, a gigantic gravity vortex, a trap that sucks Terran ships right out of space—and kills us. We can't warn our home world. More humans will come, searching for us. More humans will die—because of the M'Nae."

Tears dried on her pale cheeks and Thayenta nibbled her lip. He was asking much, begging her to span the vast gap separating their species. Too often Ken had ignored that gap, tempted to think of Thayenta as merely a lovely human woman with somewhat strange coloring, forgetting she was an alien, a telepath, that her motives might be very different from his.

It was time for truth-facing all around.

Her fingers caressed his cheek. "Ken . . . pain. Thayenta pain. Ken knows." She reacted to his sympathy for the "dead" raft, ready to forgive his species much because of one little emotion.

"That's right. When you hurt, I hurt. Humans aren't necessarily evil, Thayenta. We can learn from our mistakes. Give us a chance." Ken bent his head and peered at her closely. "Thayenta, I've got to talk to Briv. I've got to make him understand. He stopped Eads once without hurting him. If he can do it again—"

"Raft. . . ." She waved helplessly at the broken pieces.

"Teleportation," Ken insisted. He gripped her shoulders and pressed for a confession. "That way's faster, and I think you know how it's done. Don't you? I can't read your mind, but I get "vibes." You haven't told me the full story, have you?"

Thayenta looked at him anxiously, and Ken felt her tiptoeing through his brain. *You think?*

"I think that you're quite capable of teleporting humans, if you want to, and maybe yourself as well. Oh, it might take Briv's help, but you have the ability. When we were first captured, the M'Nae teleported R.C. and me. And you. . . ." He stared at her intently. "When you first showed up by the shipwreck, I thought you'd walked there, out of the mist. Now I'm not sure. If you could project your image thousands of kilometers into space, what *else* can you do?"

She darted a pink tongue between small teeth, licking her lips. Ken saw the two of them cagily circling each other, mentally.

"Thayenta, level with me," he pleaded. "Time is precious. Lives are at stake . . . Terran lives and M'Nae lives."

And at last she admitted, "It is . . . difficult. Must . . . cooperate."

"R.C. and I weren't cooperating when you teleported us," Ken argued. "But we weren't in any condition to resist, certainly. What about your ambassador? Why didn't he teleport to safety?"

"Too . . . fast," Thayenta said. "Happened too fast."

Ken nodded. That made sense. "The M'Nae didn't know about needlers, didn't realize Eads and his people were edgy, panicky because they were breaking laws. And we don't know much more about you, do we?" He took Thayenta's hands. They were cold. He gently chafed her skin, attempting to call back warmth. "Thayenta, it's got to stop. There must be no more killing on either side."

Her eyes were fathomless. As the torchlight flickered, Ken caught glimpses of her pupils shimmering in the blackness. She was an alien. Yet they could touch minds and hearts.

"You *can* teleport, can't you?" he said softly.

With obvious shame, Thayenta bowed her head. "I can . . . accept, or not."

"You mean Briv's been *trying* to teleport you out of this mess all along? And you've resisted him, refused to let him?" Ken exclaimed. He was shaken. He hadn't known she possessed that much strength. What were her motives?

She caressed his cheek again. A human gesture, but done with a M'Nae grace. "I wanted to stay with Ken." He didn't have any words. He was touched and moved and appalled at the risks she had taken on his behalf. Now she stood up, abandoning the pieces of raft. "I will accept. Now, I must. Briv is not pleased."

"I'll bet he isn't, and I'm not sure I am, either," Ken said. An apprentice in a rigid, telepathic society, she'd disobeyed orders because of Ken. It was a serious offense.

"Must go," and Thayenta pointed upstream.

"To the place where the mist begins? Why? Can't we teleport from here?" Ken asked. There was no answer—more M'Nae protocol.

She ran lightly along the bank, Ken following her. He squished through reedy low spots and irritably knocked aside low hanging willow branches. Ken lengthened his stride to match hers as she loped easily through this wet, dark world.

Only when he began floundering—beyond the light of the torch, blind in the night—did Thayenta pause. The clouds parted overhead, and the triple shadows of NE 592's moons played across her pale face eerily. Purple mist rose from the stream, from the banks, floating toward the two of them.

Here.

Did she say that, or think it to him? Quite without willing it, Ken was slipping more and more into telepathic patterns, sending and receiving mental messages. Each time he and Thayenta touched minds, it was easier. With some training, he might develop into an imitation M'Nae, though he'd probably always remain on a quite juvenile level!

But could he ever learn to develop a telepathic shield?

He touched her shoulder, orienting himself to that single lovely form in this purple mist.

A wave of vertigo struck Ken, twisting his gut.

SUDDENLY, it wasn't dark any more. The world around him dissolved into light—a brilliant, corruscating rainbow of light.

He was in the aliens' council chamber. As if he'd sucked it along with him as he'd stepped through a doorway, a few wisps of purplish fog wafted about Ken's ankles. It formed the doorway from the real world to the M'Nae fortress.

The prismatic device stood a few meters away, and beside it stood Briv. Beyond Briv, the M'Nae waited. Ken tensed. There were no longer just ten M'Nae. Now there were at least twenty aliens, a semi-circle of jewel-skinned people, spreading out behind the constantly shifting prism shape.

More of them had come through the alien matter transmitter. At this rate, their numbers would soon match that of Eads' colonists.

Thayenta sidled close to Ken and he inhaled her scent of fear. His arm swept protectively about her. Whatever happened, they would face it together.

There had been some changes, and not just in the number of M'Nae. Briv was wearing a translator—a twin to Thayenta's. He must have transmitted it from the M'Nae home planet. The device clung to mossy green threads on the chest of Briv's clothing. He crossed the chamber with long, heavy strides.

"Brace yourself, Thayenta," Ken said softly. "A hell of a lot is riding on the next few minutes."

The alien leader clamped a muffling hand over his translator and spewed a stream of M'Nae profanity at Thayenta. She trembled and Ken snapped, "Leave her alone. She did the right thing. She stuck to her job until she had all the facts. Or do the M'Nae really *want* to kill more and more humans? Do you want to drag spaceship after spaceship down by that thing?" Ken pointed accusingly at the pulsating prism.

Briv's baleful stare shifted from Thayenta to Ken. "This world is M'Nae."

Ken thrust Thayenta behind him and advanced to confront the alien leader. "As long as we're discussing land rights, it was a *Terran* who first landed on this world, Briv, a man named Noland Eads. He was here a long time ago, long before you came here with your Gera-aná."

His counterattack made Briv pause. The aliens flanking the prism were silent, expressionless, waiting for the man in charge to hand out orders.

Ken's attitude took a slight directional shift. Briv reminded him of R.C. and Eads. He was strong, even ruthless, because he had to be, carrying the weight of responsibility for so many lives. Now Ken had added more lives, Terran lives, to Briv's burden.

Ken envisioned a massed bank of telepathic claws, waiting to rake his mind to ribbons. Yes, Briv could do that, but would he?

"Try it, and I get mad," Ken said coldly. "Thayenta didn't detect those guards along the trail. Their mental level was too basic, wasn't it? And when I wanted to tear you to pieces, you didn't handle that too well, did you?"

"I controlled the chief death-bringer in his anger." Briv dropped the reminder like a bomb.

Ken tensed, thought hard. "His rage was distracted by R.C. That left him wide open. The man's not in his right mind, anyway—"

"You have your death weapon."

He had almost forgotten the weight sagging his pocket. Ken pulled out the needler, held it on his palm, considering options. How could he persuade the M'Nae of his sincerity? He felt waves of tension from the aliens watching him.

Very deliberately, Ken tossed the needler away, skittering it across the undulating white floor into the shadows, out of his reach.

The silence in the chamber was awesome. Ken waited, hardly daring to breathe. It was a big gamble. He had risked everything he had on one throw of the dice. He had risked his own life, Thayenta's, R.C.'s and Eads' and the lives of all the colonists. All hung in the balance, now that Ken had thrown away his one Terran weapon.

Briv's bony face took on a peculiar expression. If the M'Nae were human, Ken would have called it mischievous. Briv sidled another step forward, within arm's length of Ken. His full lips were pulled back in a grimace. The M'Nae version of a smile? If so, it was a nasty one, and one very suited to Briv.

Without a word, Briv swung a clumsy punch at Ken's head. He was not accustomed to this style of fighting yet he stepped into a *physical* world and left himself wide open for a counter punch.

Ken parried the blow and closed his hand over Briv's fist. His muscles strained to hold the attack in check. Briv was strong, as Ken had known from the first.

For several long moments they wrestled silently, Briv's fist in Ken's hand.

Finally, Briv drew back, let his hand fall. Ken's breath whistled out and he mopped sweat from his face and neck. He hoped this wasn't merely the first round!

Thayenta ran to Ken, slipped her small hands around his arm, clinging to him. Her elation washed against his mind. Apparently Ken had scored a telling point and had not violated the rules of the game.

Briv gestured to the prism. "Gera-ana."

"I see," Ken said, employing Briv's ritual phrase. "Your matter transmitter from your home world. How did you get it to this planet?"

Briv frowned and closed his eyes. Images rushed at Ken. He let them in. His practice with Thayenta made it easier to erase the last traces of resistance to telepathic communication. At one with Briv's mind, Ken was on another world, far from NE 592, far from any solar system yet known to Earth.

IT was a world of purple mists and moonlight, and of a darkening, rapidly dying sun.

Ken was a spectator on that other world, watching Briv and many other M'Nae deep in concentration, combining their telepathic powers for a gigantic effort beyond any single M'Nae. They were . . . moving the Gera-ana, the matter transmitter prism, moving it off their world and into space!

They sent the object through the void, across incredible gulfs, until it came to a hospitable world, a resting place suitable for M'Nae colonization.

It landed here—on NE 592.

The image shifted. Ken was back on the M'Nae's home world again. All those many aliens who had stood beside Briv, helping move the prism, all but two lay limp and still and dead on the earth.

They had died, their minds destroyed in the act of teleporting that transmitter to another planet. They had sacrificed their lives for the welfare of their people.

THE vision faded, and Ken shook himself back to present reality. "You had to leave your home world?"

Briv imitated a human nod, his strong jaw nudging toward his chest. "In four hundred valia our sun will grow cold forever. We must leave. There is only one Gera-ana. It was bought with much blood and life over the long times. And it is here."

"And the force that could move it to still another planet is depleted," Ken said, remembering the dead M'Nae. The cost was higher than the aliens could bear. They had drained their strongest and finest telepathic abilities to transport the object. This had to be it for the M'Nae. There was no other choice remaining to them.

Of course, there were variations in abilities among them, just as there were among humans. Ken thought of the difference between a Zachary or an Eads and one of those club wielding goons. If the M'Nae operated like every other intelligent species, they would send their brightest and best through the transmitter first, making sure some of their species escaped the death of their home world.

Their brightest and best, people like Thayenta and Briv! Briv was one of two survivors among the powers on M'Nae—the movers of the prism. He had come through with this first expeditionary force to the new world, putting his life on the line again, for his people.

It put Briv in new perspective for Ken. He forgave some of the harsh and cruel behavior. Briv was an alien leader desperately intent on survival for his race, one of the few leaders they had left.

There was no way Briv could have known that NE 592 had already been claimed by a Terran. Nor could he have known that this Terran would return with his followers for a rendezvous nobody wanted.

"There will be more Terrans coming, Briv," Ken warned. "If they approach this world—even by accident—they'll be caught and they'll crash." Ken indicated the prism. "The Gera-ana brings M'Nae from their home world to this one. But for Terrans it's a trap, a deadly trap. You've killed Terrans with it, and you'll kill more. They're innocent victims, like your ambassador. My people didn't know who he was. They panicked and fired. The man who did that is ill, his mind twisted."

Ken sensed emotions emanating from the M'Nae. Pity? A stricken sympathy? Eads, the Terran who'd killed the ambassador, was a man whose mind was disordered? That must have struck particularly hard at the M'Nae; they placed such reliance on the intellect.

"More Terrans," Briv said slowly. "The Gera-ana, the Iontran. . . ."

Someday Ken vowed he'd learn the specifics of those terms. But for now Ken nodded emphatically. "They will come. They will come seeking Eads. They want to cure him, heal his mind."

"How . . . how may they be stopped?" Briv had taken a giant step toward concession.

Hurriedly, Ken seized the chance. "Maybe a beacon would work. We could cannibalize some equipment to build a crude warning signal." As he considered that, inspiration came to him and he added enthusiastically, "When the Patrol ships see the beacon and park out in lunar orbit, the M'Nae could reach them—telepathically. Explain what has happened, the dangers of the Gera-ana. We can lick it, Briv! M'Nae and humans working together can lick it."

"You are not like the death bringers." It was meant as a compliment, one Ken dared not accept.

"But we are, Briv. We're just like Eads and the others. We're no different," Ken insisted. "Except that R.C. and I understand. You must make Eads understand, somehow."

Briv stepped directly into Ken's mind. There were no raking talons this time. And Ken accepted, letting the alien leader explore his thoughts at will. The sensation was unnerving. Here was an intense, very masculine personality, examining his brain. Ken felt Thayenta's hand in his and was grateful for that gentle contact with reality.

It was an experience of sharing. Briv, and now all the other M'Nae, were absorbing Ken's memories and ideas. They were doing it instantly, in a heartbeat, and making a strenuous effort to adopt the human's attitudes.

The shock of the telepathic exploration jolted Ken. With difficulty, he held his ground. He mustn't cringe away, not now, not when they were meeting him, compromising.

He hoped he was up to the job—serving as a representative for the entire Terran race!

I see.

None of the aliens uttered the simple phrase, yet Ken heard it. He didn't hear it in Terran. It wasn't possible, he couldn't understand the M'Nae language.

Good. Thayenta spoke up, telepathically. *He can be helped, become good once more.*

Eads, she was talking about curing the man. Was it possible?

Would it be in time?

R.C. Ken reached out with his thoughts. Where was R.C. right now? Was the space veteran managing okay? He was alone and wounded. Things would get rough for him if Eads' search veered toward the wrecked Class-D, as inevitably it must.

The M'Nae felt Ken's concern for the older man. They turned his anxiety over and over, examining emotions, learning about Terrans. Ken bore the invasion of privacy stolidly.

Then, abruptly, he was being carried on a beam of telepathy. It stretched out across kilometers, toward the colonists' valley, across the village, to the wrecked cargo ship.

Teleporting!

This time Ken's stomach didn't complain. He was getting used to a whole new set of physical sensations.

He moved telepathically along darkened corridors, searching for R.C.

There! Ken saw him. The pilot had managed to climb to the middle decks in the smashed hulk. And the man was hurting. He had asked too much of that wounded leg.

Voices echoed down the ship's corridors. Lights flashed in the distance. Eads and his men were closing in on the injured Surveyman.

Frustration ground at Ken. If only he were there. If only he could help R.C.!

His mind was divorced from his body, yet towing it along invisibly, like cargo. And he wasn't alone. Many other presences crowded into the wrecked space craft alongside him.

They were here in the ship. And it wasn't dark any more. With those cat's eyes of theirs, the M'Nae didn't need artificial lighting. But they provided illumination for their new Terran friends: glowing, sourceless light, like the one that had led from the prism chamber to the raft by the stream.

"What? Ken!" R.C. turned and stared at his apprentice and at the aliens accompanying him, Briv, Thayenta, and a dozen of the M'Nae.

"My escort," Ken said wryly, shifting mental gears to cope with the situation. He ran to the door of the cargo hold where R.C. had been hiding. He saw bobbing torches, down the corridor. The hunters were coming to catch their quarry—just as Ken had seen them in his mind's eye.

"Closing fast," R.C. said heavily. He leaned on a bulkhead, breathing hard. He hefted his needler and glared at it. "I hate to use this damned thing, but. . . . So far I've been able to dodge them, lead them on a wild goose chase. But it's getting harder and harder. They've got me pinned. Where's *your* needler, Ken?"

"I threw it away."

"You . . . have you gone crazy, son?" Zachary gawked at him.

Ken said quietly, "I won't need it, and you won't need yours, R.C. Briv, can you teleport all the weapons out of range? *All* the weapons—the clubs and farm tools too?"

Briv jerked his head in that characteristic M'Nae sideways nod. Down the corridor there were startled shouts, followed by silence, then a confused murmuring.

Zachary gazed at his empty hand.

"Gives you something to think about, doesn't it?" Ken said with a wry grin. "And it'll give the colonists something to think about, too, namely—just what they're up against. It's more than they can handle with brute force, and might inject a note of compromise, one we've been hoping for."

"But without weapons. . . ."

Ken went to the pilot, urging the man to sit down and rest. As R.C. submitted to Thayenta's ministrations, Ken said, "We don't need weapons. Not now. I got through to the M'Nae, R.C."

"What about their dead ambassador? asked R.C., eying Briv warily.

"He understands. And I'm beginning to," Ken said. "There's a lot yet for me to learn. But I seem to be a quick study. Maybe I have telepathic abilities. You were right, R.C. The M'Nae have power, more than we can comprehend, totally different from human technology and they're willing to work with us." Ken felt Briv and the other M'Nae brushing against his mind, taking their cues from Earth's unofficial spokesman to the alien delegation.

The mutterings of the search party had died away. Their footsteps were measured and unmenacing. R.C. tensed, waved a warning hand at Ken.

Ken shook his head, unalarmed, knowing what was coming.

Eads, his Praetorians, and several other colonists entered the cargo hold. They weren't in a trance, but their belligerence was gone. A completely different mood had taken hold of them, one of openness. They were willing to listen, to have their questions answered.

"I . . . I don't know." Noland Eads said softly. There was an uneasy stirring among his followers. Without Eads' direction, they were rudderless, and Ken conveyed that fact to the M'Nae. A few of the men were still staring wonderingly at their empty hands. Naked without their weapons, they acted without desperation. They were simply confused.

"It's okay, Captain Eads," Ken said smoothly. "There has been some confusion. That alien you met earlier was an ambassador from the M'Nae. His people would like to negotiate with you, Captain, about sharing this planet."

"Sharing?" Eads wasn't angry. In fact he looked like a man waking out of a nightmare. He shook his head slightly. "An ambassador?" Remembrance slid over his craggy features, remembrance and horror. "We . . . we killed him! My God! We killed him."

Sanity was returning to him.

"It was a mistake," Ken said. "The M'Nae understand. They'd still like to be friends. You might be interested in some of their methods of living, Captain Eads. The M'Nae live in complete harmony with nature."

"Harmony?" Eads settled on the critical point, brightening.

"That's right. They work with nature, not against it. This is Briv, the leader of the M'Nae," Ken introduced. "I'm sure he'd be glad to tell you about their clothes and rafts and other materials. They have some astonishing techniques, Captain."

He played on Eads' vulnerabilities, won his interest. And Briv made the next logical step in this sudden peace conference. His hand went out—not palm up—ready to take Eads'.

"And don't try to outgrip him," Ken warned telepathically. He noticed a slight quirk at Briv's mouth. So the M'Nae leader *did* have a sense of humor, after all!

"They're not so bad, are they?" the Praetorians were murmuring. "If they really can do things like that. . . ."

Briv didn't push it, but there *was* a small test of strength between him and Eads, a mute little challenge between two strong males of different species. It ended in a draw. Both of them backed off simultaneously. That gesture had good implications.

Eads smiled and said, "That's pretty good, friend."

"Friend," Briv repeated, not using the translator.

Eads rubbed his forehead, struggling to recall something. "It might work. It just might work. But that gravity trap of yours! We've got to stop it."

"Beacon," Briv said, picking up a word from Ken's thoughts.

"Yes, yes!" Eads bubbled with enthusiasm, addressing his men. "Of course. That's the answer. A beacon. We'll make sure nobody else gets sucked down. It'll warn them off. Don't you see, men? The M'Nae can guarantee we'll be left alone. There'll be just us, working together with nature!"

Ken eased out of the mainstream of the conversation. Eads seemed to be doing all right without further human help. He knelt beside R.C. and asked, "How's it going?"

"Not too bad, now that the war's delayed," R.C. murmured.

"Not delayed. Over."

Doubtful, R.C. eyed his old classmate. "How long can that last?"

"Leg better," Thayenta announced, patting pink fluff around R.C.'s wound. "The Chief's mind is better, too."

R.C. looked at her, then at Ken. Grinning, Ken said, "I told you she was a great little nurse. The M'Nae have a knack for medicine—and it's not limited to repairing needler wounds. Remember, R.C., they can go directly into a man's mind, and if that mind's sick, they just may be able to put it right again."

"If they can. . . ." R.C. hardly dared hope.

"Relax, R.C. you've earned a vacation." At the pilot's outraged sputtering Ken laughed, and Thayenta muffled one of those noises between a giggle and sneeze. She fully grasped the teasing going on. Ken glanced at her fondly. "Briv can handle it, now that he understands Terrans. Think of all our two peoples can learn from each other."

R.C. caught the exchange between Ken and Thayenta and rolled his eyes in exasperation. "I was talking about a war."

"Which is over." Ken chuckled and said, "Have you ever ridden a telepathic wave, R.C.? You've got something to look forward to."

R.C.'s indulgent smile reflected approval and pioneer excitement.

"It could have turned out a lot worse," Ken murmured. "For a first contact between two such disparate species."

"First contact." R.C. tasted the word, liking it.

"Let them probe your mind," Ken advised. "Don't fight them. Let them in, so they can get all they need. Don't think of it as an invasion."

"Peaceful co-existence," R.C. responded. "Terrans and M'Nae."

Ken nodded. "The M'Nae have got to come here before their sun goes cold. They're already coming through the transmitter. You can't blame them for that."

"No, certainly not."

"It will work," Ken promised.

"Easy." Thayenta spoke the word out loud and in Terran, smiling shyly at Ken.

"Right. We have a good solid beginning right here!" Ken took her small hand.

R.C. tried to ignore them, muttering to himself. "They'll have to leave that space trap transmitter of theirs in place till then. How long will that be?"

"Why, what difference does it make, Captain?" Ken said. "We *are* in Survey. Didn't you always tell me survival is our business? The first item on our agenda is exploring new worlds and new people, if we can find them, isn't it? Very few Secondary Surveymen ever have *this* kind of opportunity—discovering a whole new race of intelligent telepaths. And until they're all transmitted here from their home world, we're stuck, rooted on this planet by that gravity vortex. There's plenty of leisure time for us to get to know the M'Nae well."

R.C. sighed and conceded. Thayenta sat back on her heels, admiring her handiwork in rebandaging

R.C.'s leg. As a result of that first aid, her dress was once more reduced to an attractive, skimpy version of its former pink glory.

What had Ken told Dave Saunders back on Earth before he'd lifted ship on his way to NE 592? Survey was a soft assignment!

It was not true, of course, as this strange world had proved.

But with lovely Thayenta by his side—and he wondered if the thought were entirely his own, for she glanced at him with a special expression he hadn't seen before—he would never be able to call the years ahead the worst of times!